THE GIFT

Other books by Mona Ingram:

Brush with Destiny
But Not for Me
The Reluctant Rockstar
The Shell Game

THE GIFT

•

Mona Ingram

AVALON BOOKS

NEW YORK

Published by Avalon Books,
an imprint of Thomas Bouregy & Co., Inc.
160 Madison Avenue, New York, NY 10016

Library of Congress Cataloging-in-Publication Data

Ingram, Mona.
  The gift / Mona Ingram.
      p. cm.
  ISBN 978-0-8034-7713-1 (acid-free paper)   1. Single mothers—
Fiction.   2. British columbia—Fiction.   I. Title.
  PR9199.4.I54G54 2011
  813'.6—dc22
                                                          2010031081

PRINTED IN THE UNITED STATES OF AMERICA
ON ACID-FREE PAPER
BY HADDON CRAFTSMEN, BLOOMSBURG, PENNSYLVANIA

For Jack, with love

Chapter One

Julie paused while her eyes adjusted to the dim light. Golden afternoon sunshine filtered in through the small window at the end of the attic, illuminating the dancing dust motes. She couldn't remember the last time she'd tidied up in here, but a quick look told her that a good cleaning was long overdue. Perhaps when the tourist season was over. Right now, she had to focus on finding Nick's sleeping bag. He'd need it in a few days, and she wanted to air it out for him.

Her gaze drifted over years of accumulated clutter, then came to rest on a long, narrow box tied with what had once been a white ribbon. She reeled back, as though physically struck. How could the sight of a simple white box affect her this way? *You're in charge here*, she told herself. *All you have to do is look away.* But she didn't listen to the warning voice inside her head. It had been four years since she'd tossed that box back there, under the eaves, but in many ways it seemed like another lifetime.

"I shouldn't do this," she murmured, picking her way

1

through the debris. But the box called to her and she answered by reaching for it and blowing off the dust. She looked around for somewhere to sit, and settled for an old trunk.

The ribbon, yellowed now, slipped off easily. She hesitated. Did she want to subject herself to the memories that would be unleashed by the contents? "For heaven's sake," she said aloud. "Stop being a drama queen and either open it or put it back."

She removed the lid and placed it on the trunk beside her. Inside, white tissue paper obscured the item from view. It crackled as she folded it back to reveal her wedding veil, still pristine, still as perfect as it had been on her wedding day nine years ago.

With trembling hands, she lifted it out of the box. If only things could have turned out differently! She gave the veil a gentle shake, and several pieces of confetti drifted to the floor. On closer inspection, there were a few more pieces still caught in the delicate folds and she shook it again, recalling how the air had been filled with confetti tossed by friends and family who had helped celebrate that special day.

In those bright, happy days, anything had seemed possible. She glanced at the confetti sprinkled on the floor. So what if things hadn't worked out the way she'd imagined? *All things considered, life has been good,* she admitted with a wry smile. She returned the veil to the box and slid the ribbon back on. She briefly considered throwing it out. *But no*, she mused, placing it on a set of rough-hewn shelves. She'd keep it, if only as a reminder of how much she had changed in the intervening years.

"Aha, there you are!" she cried aloud, spotting Nick's sleeping bag. He had a bad habit of running partway up the ladder and tossing things into the attic. No wonder it was such a mess. She'd have to talk to him about that.

Back downstairs, she opened the sliding doors off the dining room and took the sleeping bag outside, shook it, and hung it over the railing. She ran her hand over the soft plaid flannel and her heart swelled with love for her son. Nick was going camping, and she could picture him snuggled down in it, sleeping around a campfire. He liked going on outings with the Cub Scouts, and she suspected that, besides the many activities, he enjoyed the attention of the men who were in charge. She sighed and went downstairs to the office.

"Did it ever occur to you how lucky you are to live right above where you work?" Julie's friend Maggie Taylor was in the office, manning the phones and doing the hundred and one things necessary to keep a houseboat charter company running.

"I can't imagine doing it any other way." Julie grinned at her friend. "Ever since I was a kid, growing up here in this house, I knew I wanted to be involved in the business. Remember how I'd collect wildflowers and put them in little vases on the houseboats? I wonder how many people with allergies threw them away as soon as they got out onto the lake."

"Doesn't matter." Maggie continued working while she talked. "I know they all appreciated those little touches of yours."

Julie walked to the wall of windows overlooking Sicamous Narrows. "I never tire of this view. Especially at this time of year." A lush green lawn sloped down toward the water, and an early summer breeze stirred the long, slender leaves of a massive weeping willow.

"That's good, since it's the only one you've ever known." Maggie joined her friend at the window, her gaze drifting over the sparkling water and the lush stands of evergreens on the hills opposite. "Seems like only yesterday that we were kids without a care, diving off the end of the dock." She gestured to the willow. "I can still remember when we stuck that willow branch into the ground and how quickly it took root. Didn't your dad give serious consideration to yanking it out?"

Julie's generous lips curved in a smile. "Yeah, but he was no match for us, thank goodness." She ran an eye over the line of houseboats rocking gently in the wake of a passing boat. "Back then he was operating Sun Bird with six houseboats. Remember?"

"Yeah, I do. He and your mom would get excited every time they got a booking." She made a broad gesture. "And now look. Twenty-two houseboats, of which two are eight-sleepers and the rest twelve. All equipped with waterslides, hot tubs, barbecues, and television." She glanced at Julie. "You've done really well, you know? I don't tell you that enough."

"Thanks, Mags." Julie's gaze shifted to the fleet of houseboats moored along the dock directly to the west. "But there's just one fly in the ointment."

Her friend's eyes narrowed. "They're still giving you a hard time, huh?"

"Oh, yeah. Big time." She glared down at the neighboring company. Not for the first time, she wished that her father had purchased a bigger piece of land. But she couldn't fault him for that. Back then, no one had foreseen the explosion in demand for houseboat vacations here in British Columbia.

When other companies started up, they had recognized the desirability of Sicamous Narrows. There was now a string of houseboat companies on the stretch of water connecting Mara Lake with sprawling, many-armed Shuswap Lake.

Julie walked over to her desk. "After you went home yesterday, they sent over one of their flunkies with a message." She riffled through the papers on her desk. "I can't find it right now, but it said they wanted to inform me that they were surveying."

"A land survey?" Maggie frowned. "Why?"

"Mainly to try to intimidate me, I think. It wasn't necessary to inform me they're doing it, even if they are our neighbors." She was almost sputtering with outrage. "Since when have they ever been neighborly? No, they sent the note to needle me." She ran her fingers through her hair, and it sprang right back. "How many times do I have to tell them I don't want to sell my company, or my land?"

"A few more times, I suppose." Maggie shrugged. "But you're in the driver's seat, so try not to let them get to you."

"Yeah, but stealing my staff is dirty pool, Mags. You notice they only poach the ones who've been trained."

"You'll find more, never fear. Carl and Jenna will whip them into shape in no time." Maggie's niece was in charge of the crew of young people who cleaned the houseboats, and Carl had worked for SunBird since Julie's parents' time.

"I suppose you're right." She gave her friend what she hoped was a bright smile. "Listen, if you're going to the bank and to the post office, why don't you leave now and take the rest of the day off? We have nobody scheduled to come back in today, and no rentals going out. I'm going to do some touch-up painting on the boats."

"Isn't that Carl's job?"

Julie grinned. "Yeah, but you know how I like to be involved in the hands-on stuff. Besides, he's servicing the motors on *Osprey* and *Goldeneye*."

"Okay, then." Maggie gathered up the stack of envelopes and the deposit book. "See you tomorrow, kiddo."

Julie watched her friend walk toward the SunBird Charters parking lot. She was lucky to have a friend who was not only loyal but also smart. Maggie favored bright colors, fringed scarves, and long, flowing skirts. Today, her russet hair was pinned up with her trademark black-lacquered chopsticks. If asked, Maggie would have described herself as "generously proportioned," but to Julie's eyes she was the Maggie she'd always known and loved. Her tongue might have been sharp, but her mind was sharper. It was Maggie who had insisted around twelve years ago that they "get with it" and install the latest Internet software.

She watched her friend pull out of the parking lot, then ran back upstairs to change into a faded pair of cut-offs.

Julie shook out the sleeping bag once more and flipped it over. Nick had promised to come home in time to give her a hand with some chores, but as long as he was back in time for dinner, it didn't really matter. The chores weren't really necessary; they were her way of instilling a sense of responsibility in her son, and so far it seemed to be working. She ran lightly down the two sets of stairs and across the lawn.

She smiled to herself as she passed empty spaces on either side of the dock. About half the fleet was somewhere out on the lake, occupied by customers taking advantage of the shoulder season rates. Many were seniors who visited the area every year, eager to get out on the pristine waters of Shuswap Lake. The remainder of the fleet rocked silently at their moorings, waiting for the onset of the summer season.

Shuswap Lake seemed to have been designed for houseboats. Sprawled in an area just north of the Okanagan Valley in British Columbia, it resembled a drunken, irregular *H* resting on its side with stubby little "feet" at the west end, or bottom, of the *H*. Sandy beaches approved for public use dotted the shoreline, and most renters motored placidly during the day, pulling into one of the sites in the evening.

A grizzled head popped up through the hatch on the back deck of *Osprey*. "Oh, it's you, Julie. I thought I heard someone." Carl Morrison had been maintenance supervisor of SunBird Charters since Julie's father's time. What Carl didn't know about the houseboats wasn't worth knowing. Quiet and competent, he rarely voiced an opinion, but if he did, Julie always listened.

"Oh, hi, Carl. I'm going to touch up the rails on *Swallow*." She paused. "Any problems?"

"Nope." He wiped his sweaty forehead with the arm of his shirt. "There's an open can of that dark blue paint in the maintenance shed, and paint thinner on the shelf right beside it." His eyes sparkled. Many years ago, Julie had neglected to clean out a paintbrush, and he'd never let her forget it.

"Thanks for reminding me. I might have forgotten." Julie gave him her standard answer and they both laughed. The rear decks of the houseboats took a lot of hard wear. The boats were backed into the dock, where the gate in the railing could be opened for loading supplies. The gas barbecue also sat on the back deck, which was large enough to accommodate several folding chairs. What with all the activity, the rails seemed to be constantly in need of repainting.

Julie hummed to herself as she worked along the side railings. She glanced at her watch. Nick should be here soon; she'd better decide what chore to give him. She went down on her knees, reaching behind the barbecue. It was bolted to the floor, making it awkward to get to the rails behind it, but she'd been doing this for more years than she cared to count, and knew that it wasn't worth the time it took to unbolt it and move it out of the way. She angled her body behind the barbecue, moved the paint can to a more convenient position, and started to paint the underside of the railing. Out of the corner of her eye she noticed the dock dip, and the movement was followed by the soft, familiar sound of water slapping against the bottom of the float.

A blob of dark blue paint fell to the deck and she groaned, angry with herself for allowing her attention to wander.

"Now look what I've done." Julie's voice was testy. "Hand me that rag, would you, Nick?" She stuck out her hand behind her and the rag was placed wordlessly in her palm. "You'd think I'd never done this before."

"Hi, Jules." His words cut through her mounting tirade and her heart did a quick little tap dance against her ribs. It couldn't be! But his voice was unforgettable.

She twisted her head very slowly and looked sideways at the dock. The lower portion of a pair of muscled legs filled her vision, as tanned as her own despite the fact that summer had barely started. One foot, clad in a dark sandal, rested on the low railing, and he leaned forward to peer at her. A heart-stopping grin spread slowly over his face and Julie squeezed her eyes shut, quite sure that when she opened them he would have vanished.

"What are you doing down there on your hands and knees?"

He was real! Her eyes snapped open and her head jerked up, clipping the underside of the barbecue with a sharp rap.

"Ow!" she cried, scrambling to her feet.

He stepped onto the houseboat and held her gently by the arm. "I'm sorry, Julie. I should have announced myself, but you looked so darned cute down there."

"Quentin." She looked up at him and her breath caught in her throat. How many times over the past sixteen years had she thought about him, wondered if he'd achieved his goals, if he was happy? Did he know how she'd ached when he left, even though there'd been nothing serious between them? She gave her head a quick shake.

"I thought you were Nick. He said he'd be back about now, and when I saw the dock move I thought it was him. He promised to give me a hand around here this afternoon. You could have said something, you know." She was babbling, and stopped abruptly to look at him again.

His eyes held hers, and for a moment they were suspended in time, openly assessing each other.

The years since their last meeting melted away as she searched his face for changes. If anything, he was more handsome, although when she'd last seen him she hadn't thought that would be possible. Of course a man was bound to change in sixteen years, but his eyes sparkled with the same mix of intelligence and humor. His dark blonde hair had been professionally styled, but it was windblown now, threatening to revert to its former unruly state if left untended too long. She smiled at the thought.

"So you came back," she whispered, a hint of wonder in her voice. "It's good to see you, Quentin." The houseboat rocked gently as a powerboat glided past the end of the dock, but Julie scarcely noticed. She watched curiously as he moved to the deck and wet his handkerchief under the hose bib. His movements were quietly confident and he wrung it out as he approached her, eyes on her forehead. He slid his hand around the back of her neck, sending little sparks of electricity shooting through her veins.

"You've got a black smudge on your forehead. Let me wipe it off for you."

Julie lowered her head, fearing that if she looked into his eyes she would be completely lost.

"There, that's just about got it. Now let me look at your head and see if you did any damage."

His hands were strong and sure as he inspected the top of her head. She was close enough to smell his aftershave. It was subtle, and probably expensive, but then, if he wore paint thinner it would probably smell good to her. Swaying slightly, she backed up against the barbecue, reluctant to admit that her slight dizziness had more to do with the way his hands caressed her head than anything else.

"You'll have a bit of a lump, but that's all." His smile was reassuring.

"That's good to know." She raised her fingers to her head, touching the spot with probing fingers. She was starting to get a headache. "When did you get back?"

"Just today, as a matter of fact. You see, I—"

They both turned as a young boy came hurtling down the short ramp and onto the dock. "Hey, Mom. Tommy and I caught some fish! It was totally cool. We went out in the boat with his dad and . . ." He stopped short, sending a curious glance from his mother to the stranger leaning against the railing. He smiled politely and started to back away.

"That's okay, Nick. He isn't a customer. This is Quentin

Callahan. He grew up here in Sicamous. He was a friend of your uncle Mike's." She leaned forward and spoke in a loud whisper. "He used to hang around our house all the time. Quite a pest, to tell you the truth."

Quentin pushed away from the railing and stepped forward, hand outstretched. After a moment's hesitation, Nick extended his hand, trying to appear nonchalant.

"Good to meet you, Nick." Quentin shot Julie a wry glance. "But let's set the record straight here. It was your mother who was the pest back then, not me."

Nick's gaze darted from one adult to the other, amused by the friendly banter. If this man thought he was going to get the better of his mom, he had another thing coming. But it would be fun to watch him try. "So I guess not much has changed," he said with a cheeky grin.

"Nicholas Chapman, you're treading on thin ice here," Julie scolded, but she could not hide her smile. "And anyway, I thought you were going to help me out around here for a while this afternoon."

Nick sobered. "Sorry, Mom. I didn't tell Tommy's dad what time I had to be back, and he took us out farther than I realized. What would you like me to do?"

"Drain the hot tub on *Pintail* for me, would you? They say they didn't use it, but give it a brush with the disinfectant anyway, and then refill it." She gestured back up the ramp to the parking lot. "And then could you straighten out the carts for me? They've left them all over the place today, as usual."

Nick loved driving the small ATVs with carts that were used by the customers to bring supplies from their vehicles down to the docks. Julie gave him every opportunity to drive them on the property as a bonus for helping out with the more mundane chores.

"Anything else, Mom?" He seemed keen to get started, and Julie frowned.

"No, that's all. Why?"

The youngster kicked his sneaker against the low railing that ran along the edge of the dock. "I was wondering if I could go back to Tommy's house later. His dad invited me to dinner." His eyes danced in anticipation. "They're ordering pizza because Tommy's mom works late tonight. Can I go . . . please?"

Julie sighed, then ruffled the boy's hair. He squirmed uncomfortably and shot an embarrassed glance in Quentin's direction. "All right. What are you doing after dinner?"

"We'll probably head over to the ballpark and knock some balls around. I'll be home by nine, as usual."

"Okay, then." She turned to Quentin as her son hurried off. "I don't know where he gets the energy, but I'd rather see him active than sitting around the house playing video games."

Quentin looked after the young boy. "He seems like a nice kid, but then I wouldn't have expected anything else. Besides, I recall someone else who was full of energy when she was young."

"I was, wasn't I?" She drew in a deep breath and let it out slowly. "I wish I had more of that energy these days. I really thought that running this business would get easier as time went along, but it hasn't. Quite the opposite, as a matter of fact. There are always new problems to be solved." She gave her head a quick shake. "But enough about me. What are you doing back here? I don't even know where you're living right now."

"Let's just say I'm taking a time-out." He looked past the row of houseboat companies that lined the Narrows to the low hills that surrounded the lake. "I don't think I realized how much I missed this place." He looked down at her. "Speaking of time-out, are you expecting any more customers today?"

"Nope. Everybody showed up at once today. Returns as well as outgoing. It was a bit hairy for a while." She made a soft sound of annoyance. "I don't know why we bother to give them a schedule for arrivals and departures, because they don't stick to it." She waved a hand in front of her face. "Sorry for venting. You were asking about customers?"

"Yeah. If you have no further commitments, I thought maybe we could go out and get a bite of dinner together. You could bring me up to speed on the old hometown. That is, unless you have other plans?"

It didn't take her long to make up her mind. She hadn't dated since the divorce, but this wasn't really a date . . . was it? What harm could there be in having a quick bite to eat with an old family friend? She had her emotions under control now—he'd caught her by surprise, that was all. No more racing heartbeat or wobbly legs. He was her brother's friend, for goodness sake!

She glanced at her watch. "Could you give me an hour? I have to lock up here and check the books for what's happening tomorrow." *And fix my hair, add a dab of cologne, and change clothes.* "Where do you want to go?"

"Anywhere is fine with me. You choose."

"Something simple. Let's go to the place by the old Railway Bridge. We can sit outside. See you in an hour, okay?"

He nodded agreement and sauntered up the dock, hands

in his pockets. At the head of the ramp he turned and glanced back to where she stood, watching him. With a small wave he ducked under the willow tree and disappeared from sight, leaving her wondering how on earth she'd be able to concentrate on work for the next hour.

Chapter Two

So how is Mikey these days?" They sat on opposite sides of a picnic table on the outside deck of the restaurant.

"When was the last time you saw him?" She thought she knew, but she'd like to hear him say it.

"About sixteen years ago." He looked at her steadily over the rim of his coffee cup.

She allowed herself a sad little smile. "I haven't seen him for almost a year. It's too long. They live up at Williams Lake and he has a management position at the mill. You remember how he loved the outdoors when we were kids? Well, they have a small acreage with a few cattle and some horses. Sharon says he's really content. I'm happy for him."

"Me too. It's too easy for people to get stuck in jobs they don't really like, but they feel trapped and don't know how to change."

"It sounds like you may have some firsthand experience with that."

He nodded his head slowly while his eyes followed a large houseboat sliding under the bridge and into the main body of the lake. "Yes, I suppose I do." He continued to watch the houseboat. "Look at the size of that thing!"

Julie turned sideways on the bench and followed his gaze. "That's a sixteen-sleeper. It belongs to Apex Houseboats. Not my favorite people right about now."

His head snapped around. "Why not?"

She stared into her coffee cup for a while before raising her eyes to meet his. "I don't know if I want to get into that tonight. Let's talk about something pleasant. Oh, look. Our burgers are here already."

"There you go." The waitress placed a large platter in front of each of them and set a bowl of rich brown gravy on the table between them. "I'll be right back with some more coffee."

Julie spooned some gravy over her fries and popped one into her mouth. "Ahh," she sighed. "I don't care how much fat these things contain, or calories either. They taste good."

Quentin raised his eyebrows. "Trust me, Jules. You have no problems in that department."

"Thanks," she said, picking up her burger. "You just made my day. So, tell me everything. How long are you here for and what have you been doing with yourself all this time?"

"Give me a minute to enjoy this thing, would you?" They ate in silence for a few moments, content in each other's company.

Quentin finished first and wiped his fingers on a napkin. "You seem stronger, Julie," he said abruptly.

"Be still my heart." She tried to glare at him but only succeeded in wrinkling her eyebrows. "You really know how to flatter a girl."

He laughed and reached across the table, brushing the back of her hand with long, sensitive fingers. "It was meant to be a compliment, you know."

She rolled her eyes. "Well, all right then. Now, come on. Tell me what you've been up to."

Quentin gave the waitress a dazzling smile as she refilled his cup, then he turned his attention back to Julie. "I don't know if you remember, but when I left here I was focused on getting an education." He paused. "Determined to succeed."

His words stung. Did he really think she would have forgotten that night? She hid behind her coffee mug.

"When I got down to the coast, I studied for the next four or five years nonstop. I had a job, of course, so my life consisted of work and study, work and study. I had very little time for anything else. I took an accelerated course in business administration and specialized in finance. I soaked it all up like a sponge—at least that's what my professors said." He tapped his fingernails against the side of his coffee mug and looked off into the distance. "One of the companies I interned with gave me some assignments and I found that I was particularly adept at assessing the strengths and weaknesses of a business. They wanted to hire me right out of school, which was flattering, but that wasn't what I wanted. I'd worked too hard, and above all I was determined to be independent." He paused, and a shadow flitted across his eyes. "Things weren't easy at home when I was growing up, and I think that influenced me more than I realized. So I set up my own consulting firm, and I'm happy to say I haven't looked back."

"So where does your business come from? Who hires

you?" Julie leaned forward, fascinated by this new Quentin who spoke with such authority.

"Sometimes a company will hire me as a pair of 'outside eyes' to come in and work with their people, then provide them with a report on their internal structure. I make recommendations, and point out where they can improve their operations." He grinned. "I like that part of the business because it's positive. But mostly, I work for one large corporation that expands by buying other companies. When they target a company, they hire me to assess it for weaknesses that they can exploit when they go after it. It's accepted practice in the world of business, but between you and me, it's the least palatable part of what I do." He paused. "Recently I've suspected that some of their dealings aren't exactly ethical."

"But this company is a big percentage of your business." Julie watched him intently.

Her quick grasp of his dilemma was impressive. "Yes, but I'd rather do without their business than work for people I don't respect. So . . . I've decided to step back from it for a while." He spread his hands, palms up. "And here I am. I've been planning this break for over a year and I've got a whole month to myself."

Julie sighed. "A whole month. I envy you. What are you going to do?"

Quentin's gaze went back to the water, then touched on the railway bridge before returning to her face. "I'm going to decompress for a few days, then I'll visit my dad. I don't know if you were aware of this when we were kids, but Dad and I didn't get along very well."

"I sort of figured that out from a few things Mike said." Julie didn't know what else to say.

"I realize now that it couldn't have been easy for him after Mom died." His fingers tightened around his coffee mug. "But other people have lived through loss without becoming alcoholics. Let's just say he wasn't much of a father figure."

Julie nodded. "Where is he now? I'm ashamed to say I don't even know."

He gave his head a quick shake. "Don't think that. I doubt you ever met him."

"No, I didn't actually."

"Well, he's recently moved to a seniors care facility in Vernon, so I'd like to check it out as well as see him."

"So where are you staying?"

"I'm in that new motel down on the beach at Mara Lake. It's comfortable, and peaceful too. It will give me time to work myself up to seeing Dad."

"Good idea," she mused. "So, I guess you noticed all the new places along Mara Lake."

"I wouldn't have recognized it. When I left, there were only a couple of motels, but now the entire shoreline is studded with resorts and campgrounds."

"Sixteen years can bring a lot of changes." Julie gestured over her shoulder. "What about all the houseboat companies? There are over a dozen of us now."

"That's progress, I guess." In the evening twilight, hundreds of houseboats and pleasure craft rode at anchor, strung out along the Narrows. "I remember when there was just your mom and dad's company and a couple of other people who rented out their own boats." He waved off the waitress, who was offering coffee refills. "You've done an amazing job, Julie, building up the company the way you have."

She shot him a curious look. "How do you know that,

Mr. Big-Time Vancouver Financial Expert? How do you know it was me?"

He leaned forward on his elbows. "Because I get the local newspapers, Miss Smarty Pants. I may have left here all those years ago, but I've never forgotten about the place." His eyes held hers. "The good memories, as well as the bad."

"Oh." It was disconcerting, the way he could make her feel like a young girl again.

"So where are your parents now?" he asked. "I recall reading about a big retirement party, but that was years ago, wasn't it?"

"They live on the Island now." Julie's voice softened as she spoke of her parents. "They spend the summers at home in Qualicum Beach, and in the winter they usually spend five months in Arizona. They've earned their retirement, no doubt about that."

"Do they come back and visit often?"

"They come at least once a year." Julie grinned. "They love their grandson, and he's crazy about them, of course. Dad had a small heart attack shortly after they left here, but he's much better now. He walks every day along the waterfront, and they play a lot of golf."

The sun had set while they were eating, and Julie shivered as a light breeze fluttered the umbrella over their table. "The evenings aren't all that warm yet. As usual, I'm rushing the season." She rubbed her bare arms, and Quentin rose from his side of the table.

"Come on, let's take a drive around town. We can check on Nick while we're at it."

He slipped his arm around her shoulders and she had a

sudden urge to lean into him and absorb his strength. It had been a long time since a man had protected her, cherished her. Startled at the direction of her thoughts, she gave him a weak smile as they headed toward his car.

"Shall I put the top up?" he asked, his eyes reflecting his concern. The dark blue Mercedes convertible had drawn a few covetous glances on the drive over to the restaurant.

"I'll be fine," she said, slipping into the luxurious leather seat.

He reached into the back and pulled out a jacket. "Here, then. Let me put this around your shoulders." His fingers brushed against her neck, and her skin ignited from his touch.

He walked around the back of the car, his stride quiet and confident. She squeezed her eyes shut, fighting for control of her emotions. The door closed with a soft thud as he eased into the driver's seat.

"Nice car," she murmured, casting a sidelong glance at his profile. "Your business must be doing well."

He backed out of the parking spot and grinned. "You could say that. I may not always enjoy what I do, but it's very rewarding."

His right cheek dimpled, and Julie was glad she was buckled in, otherwise she might have leaned across and kissed him. Right there, on the dimple. "All that success might make it hard to give up . . . if that's what you decide."

"Yes and no." His face turned serious. "I can afford to slow down a bit. Cherry-pick the jobs I want to do. I mean, how much money does one guy need, anyway? I'm no Bill Gates, but I've made some excellent investments, and I have a bit stashed away. I'll always work at something."

He drove in silence toward the ballpark and pulled up in the parking lot beside the backstop.

"There he is." Julie pointed through the windshield. "He's playing with Tommy and Ryan." She watched for a few moments as Nick caught a fly ball and threw it back to Ryan. "I don't know much about that kid," she said, almost to herself. "His family moved here around a year ago and he's awfully quiet, but Nick seems to like him."

Nick spotted them and waved, but continued playing.

"I guess it wouldn't be appreciated if we offered to drive him home?" Quentin mused.

Julie laughed. "Definitely uncool. Anyway, they brought their bikes." Two bikes leaned against the backstop. "I'm not sure if Ryan has one, but I think he only lives a few blocks away."

Quentin drove slowly through the small town and Julie pointed out the changes. They were soon pulling into the parking lot of SunBird Charters.

"Home again," sighed Julie as she surveyed the boats lined up along the dock. It was peaceful now in the gathering darkness and they walked down onto the sloping lawn. She pulled his jacket tighter around her shoulders and sat on an old rock wall that her father had built to encircle the willow tree. The rocks still held the warmth of the sun.

"Why did you show up here today, Quentin?" She cocked her head to one side and looked up at him as he leaned against the wall beside her. *If I didn't know this man*, she thought idly, *I'd think he was too handsome to be real*. And, if she were honest with herself, she'd admit that her attraction to him was more than that of an old family friend.

A puzzled grin flashed across his face. "I don't know. Somehow it just seemed right." He looked down at her. "Old habits die hard, I guess." He craned his neck and looked over at the rental company to her left. "That's Apex House-boats, huh? You mentioned something about them earlier. Have they been giving you problems?"

Julie looked over at the adjoining set of docks. Apex had opted for a sleek, edgy look in boat design as well as interior décor. Their color scheme relied on a lot of grays and blacks, accented by dark blue and maroon. She'd often thought that even their boats were vaguely threatening when compared to the light, airy colors she'd chosen as her color scheme.

"It all started in the middle of last season, when they made an offer to buy me out." Her gaze came back to her own fleet and she smiled with pride. "Of course I refused. I love this spot, even though it's not big enough for me any-more."

"Really?" Quentin frowned.

She made an impatient gesture toward the dock. "See for yourself. I've extended the dock as far as the by-laws allow. I can't expand my fleet. If I want to buy a new boat, I have to get rid of one." She swung her legs, kicking her heels against the rock wall. "But to get back to Apex, I don't like to sound paranoid, but ever since I turned them down, I've been having problems." She gave him a tentative look. "Small things, you know. Like they keep hiring my people. They've got more staff over there than they can possibly use and they still offer my trained staff more money to work for them. You can't blame the kids for leaving when it's two or three dollars an hour more than I can pay them." She shook her head. "And my signs are always 'blowing' down. Even when there's no wind, they mysteriously end up facedown out by the road frontage. Little things like that, but what I really worry about is that they'll damage one of the houseboats, and a customer could be placed in danger. It would be so easy to put a small hole in one of the pontoons. That could ruin somebody's trip, not to mention give us a lot of grief."

"Did they make you an offer in writing?" He eased away from the wall and stood beside her, suddenly very businesslike.

"No, I told them not to bother." She paused. "They approached me twice, as a matter of fact, and I told them both times that I wasn't interested in selling."

He applauded softly. "Good for you, Jules. I always knew you could stick up for yourself."

She nodded, but she hadn't finished venting. "What's worse, it's not even owned by a local company. It's some big conglomerate from the coast. No community involvement whatsoever."

Quentin took in the houseboats lined up along the dock next door and his eyes narrowed. "Maybe they'll leave you alone when it gets busier in a couple of weeks."

"I sure hope so. One of my students gave notice today. We had just finished training him for maintenance, too. Thank goodness for Carl Morrison." She glanced toward the maintenance shed at the end of the dock. "You probably remember him. He was here when you and Mike used to help out, and he's worth three men. And as for the cleaning crew, Maggie's two nieces are very reliable, so we're managing."

"So Maggie's still around, then?"

Julie grinned and nodded her head. "Maggie and I will be friends forever, I think. She runs the office and handles the incoming guests. She says it gives her a chance to check out the men. She's still hopeful, in spite of the fact that she got divorced for the second time last year."

"Can't wait to see her. Does she still wear those wild clothes?"

"Quentin Callahan, are you criticizing my best friend?" Julie's voice was teasing. She hopped down from the wall. "Let's just say she still dresses with flair, but the customers don't seem to mind." She glanced at her watch. "Nick should be home any minute, and as soon as he settles down, I'm going to crash. I have to get up early and help Carl with some oil changes. We need to prep three boats before noon tomorrow."

Quentin's mouth slid into a lopsided grin and Julie's eyes were once again drawn to the dimple in his cheek. "I think that's a hint for me to leave," he drawled. He reached down and grasped her hand, bringing it slowly to his mouth. His lips were soft against her fingers and he held her eyes with his. "Thank you for tonight, Julie. I enjoyed every minute."

Rooted to the spot, Julie couldn't form a coherent thought. The low, throaty rumble of an inboard motor echoed the frantic beating of her heart as he lowered his head. His lips brushed her cheek so briefly that she might have imagined it, but for the sudden jolt of longing that coursed through her veins.

He gave her hand a gentle squeeze, then stepped back. "Good night, Squirt."

The use of her childhood nickname brought her suddenly back to earth. "Good night yourself," she called as he walked toward the parking lot.

She walked unsteadily up the front stairs to the house. *I'm a mother and a successful businesswoman, not an inexperienced teenager*, she told herself, settling down in a chair on the sundeck. His jacket was still around her shoulders and she buried her nose in it, breathing in his scent. She was transported back to that night sixteen years ago. The night of her high school graduation.

Chapter Three

Julie and her mother had visited all the stores in the nearby town of Salmon Arm before deciding on a pale yellow dress for the graduation dance. She did not have a steady boyfriend and had been surprised when Boyd Charles asked her to the dance. He picked her up in his father's car, and in her new dress and upswept hair she felt very grown up as she waved good-bye to her parents, Boyd's corsage of white roses pinned to her dress.

The high school gym had been transformed. Julie was on the decorating committee and had worked until late that afternoon, but seeing it now, with the lights dimmed, it was even better than she had anticipated. Helium-filled balloons bobbed in clusters around the tables, upon which clusters of candles cast flickering light. Suspended over the dance floor, twinkling lights created a starry canopy. The obligatory crepe paper streamers in the school colors brightened the walls and the stage, where a band played energetically.

Julie's class was small, with only thirty-eight graduates. They exchanged partners and danced almost nonstop, pausing only to drink from the punch bowl that was guarded by one of the teachers.

During a break in the music, she looked around for Boyd and spotted him coming in from outside with two other boys. He appeared slightly rumpled, but waved off her concerns. As the night went on, he danced less and less, sitting sprawled at the table, watching the dancers with a belligerent expression on his face.

Julie watched him nervously, and decided to call it a night. "I'd like to go home now, Boyd." She stood in front of him and forced herself to smile. The magic had gone out of the evening, and she struggled to hold back tears.

"Oh you would, would you?" He lurched up and took her arm, propelling her out to the parking lot. "That's fine with me." He opened the car door and handed her in roughly, slamming the door behind her. He pulled out of the parking lot with a squeal of tires and headed in the opposite direction from her house.

Her uneasiness turned to fear. "Where are you going?" she asked, trying not to sound worried. "This isn't the way to the Narrows."

He curled his lip. "I know that, but first I want to show you one of my favorite spots." He swerved and missed an oncoming car by a few feet, then pulled off abruptly onto a side road.

Julie knew it led to a parking lot beside a small lake. Her schoolmates usually giggled when they talked about parking there with their boyfriends. She edged over toward the window, putting as much space between herself and her date as she could.

Boyd lunged at her as soon as the car stopped. "Come on, Julie. Just a little kiss." His fingers clawed at the French twist that had made her feel so grown-up just a few hours before. The hairpins scattered, and her hair fell around her shoulders.

"Come on, Julie," he said, grabbing at her dress. The pin from her corsage stabbed his fingers and he recoiled with a cry. The shoulder of her dress had slipped down her arm, but she didn't notice. She grabbed her evening bag, scrambled out of the front seat as quickly as she could, and ran back toward the highway. Boyd stumbled out of the car and yelled after her. Then she heard a retching sound and realized he was being sick. She kept on running toward the highway and was momentarily blinded by headlights. She put up her hand to shield her eyes as the car came to a halt.

The driver got out. "Julie, is that you?"

She recognized Quentin's voice. He ran toward her and gathered her in his arms. She leaned into him, limp with relief. "Are you all right?" He adjusted the sleeve of her dress. "Do you have a jacket?" He realized she'd been crying and brushed a tear from her cheek. She shook her head.

He strode back to his car and pulled out a jacket, draping it over her shoulders. She smiled up at him through the tears. "I'm sorry, Quentin. I should have realized that he'd been drinking. I wouldn't have asked him to drive me home if I hadn't been so naïve."

He gave her a gentle shake. "Listen here, Squirt. Don't go blaming yourself for this. I'd like to go back there right now and straighten him out, but I'm more concerned with you. What do you say we clean you up a bit and go out for a snack?" He bent his knees and peered closely into her eyes. "That will give you time to recover before I take you home. Okay?"

Julie nodded. "That would be nice. Thanks."

En route to the local diner she composed herself, but she was relieved to see that they were the only customers when he pulled up outside the old railway car. He settled her in a booth and went to the counter to place their order. He'd been two years ahead of her in school, and he'd left town right after graduation. He appeared taller than before, and his shoulders filled the soft denim shirt he wore tucked into a pair of jeans. He was a man now, she realized. A very attractive man.

He came back to the booth followed by the waitress bearing a tray with coffee and banana cream pie. Julie didn't have the heart to tell him that she hadn't yet acquired a taste for coffee.

"So," she said, stirring some sugar into her coffee. "What have you been doing since you and Mike graduated?" She took a gulp of coffee.

"I've been working at the mill, plus taking some correspondence courses at the same time." He glanced around the diner, as though committing it to memory. "I'm leaving for Vancouver in the morning."

She paused, a forkful of pie partway to her mouth. "You must be awfully determined to do both at the same time. Mike's working at a mill up in Williams Lake and he says it's a tough job."

Quentin shrugged. "Yeah, but you get used to it. My goal is to get my master's in business administration, and this is the way to fast-track it."

"I'm impressed."

He reached into his pocket for a coin and flipped through the list of songs on the jukebox. He punched D14, and music filled the diner.

"How is Mike, anyway? I haven't seen him since school." The silky voice of Nat King Cole flowed around them, singing the familiar lyrics of "When I Fall in Love."

"He's doing great. He has a girlfriend, and I wouldn't be surprised if they get married." She looked at him shyly. "How about you? Do you have a girlfriend?" She crossed her fingers under the table, praying for the right answer.

"No time for that, I'm afraid. My studies are taking up all my spare time right now."

Julie nodded, trying to appear wise. Why hadn't she ever noticed how handsome he was? His sandy hair was cropped close to his head, and she had an almost uncontrollable urge to reach out and touch the stubble on the square lines of his jaw. And his lips! They were full and sensuous, and she found herself wondering what it would be like to kiss him.

She was being ridiculous. He was Mike's friend, nothing more. She searched her mind for something to say . . . something to occupy the sudden silence.

"When I left home tonight I had my hair up. I'll tell Mom that the pins came out."

He pushed his plate away, the pie half eaten, and studied her as though seeing her for the first time. "You look lovely, Julie." His voice was oddly husky. He held out his hand. "Come on, I'll take you home now."

She wished their time together would never end. It was the first time she'd been attracted to a man, and as they drove through the silent streets, she knew that she would remember every moment of this night for a long time to come.

He pulled into the parking lot and ran around to open her door. The halogen lights bathed them both in a pink glow and he took her hand and guided her toward the stairs leading up to her family's living quarters.

They paused at the foot of the stairs. "I'm sorry your night was spoiled, Julie. You deserve better, but I want you to remember that it wasn't your fault."

She nodded, trying to memorize the way he looked. He was leaving tomorrow, and she didn't know when she would see him again.

"And one more thing." His voice was so low she leaned forward, not wanting to miss a word. "You've turned into a beautiful woman."

Why had she found him now? Now, when it was too late? His fingers released hers, and she muffled a small cry of anguish. As though sensing her distress he reached for her, pulling her into the circle of his arms.

"Julie," he whispered, and she looked into his eyes. He lowered his head . . . slowly, tentatively . . . and she raised her lips. His mouth covered hers, softly, gently, expertly. Her arms slipped around his neck, and with a soft moan she leaned into him, dizzy with the unfamiliar sensations that swirled through her body. Her eyes fluttered open to see him watching her intently before he broke away, taking a sharp breath. "I shouldn't have done that." His eyes glittered and, inexperienced as she was, Julie was aware of the degree of control he had just exhibited. The corner of his mouth lifted in a heart-stopping grin. "But I'm glad I did." She smiled shyly and raised two fingers to his lips.

"Me, too. Good night, Quentin, and thank you for rescuing me."

Quentin watched her run lightly up the stairs, his heart still pounding. Halfway up she paused and looked back. He raised a hand in farewell and she looked down at him for a long moment, then turned away and continued on more slowly. Light spilled out into the soft summer night as she opened the door. He waited until the door closed and the outside light was flicked off. Then he trudged back to the parking lot and climbed into his car.

Thank goodness he'd turned around when that car had almost sideswiped him on the highway. He hadn't recognized Julie or her date, but some instinct had warned him to investigate. And there she'd been, caught in the headlights of his car, and he couldn't believe his eyes. Partly because of the tears running down her face, but also because of the way she'd changed in the two short years since he'd last seen her. He smiled to himself. The interesting thing was, she didn't seem to be aware of how attractive she was. That only added to her appeal.

For the first time in many years, his resolve wavered. He'd had his share of girlfriends, but none had made him feel the way Julie just had. In the past, she'd always been Mike's little sister. Always hanging around the houseboats, cleaning and fussing while he and Mike did the minimum amount of work required.

But she'd turned into a beauty, even with her dress awry and tears streaming down her cheeks. Now she took his breath away.

He stared at the row of aspen trees lining the parking lot, their leaves stirred by a sudden breeze. Much as he'd like to pursue a relationship with Julie, he couldn't abandon his dream of becoming a successful businessman. The past two years since his own graduation had taught him a lot. He recognized that his passion, his drive, stemmed from his upbringing. After his mother's death, he'd been left to fend for himself. He'd watched his father spiral downward, becoming an alcoholic. In his early teens he'd rebelled, skipping school and roaming around the small town at all hours of the day and night. But it had been a lonely existence, and he soon found himself back in school, befriended by Mike, and taken in by the Sandersons. Mike's mom had often called him her third child as he ate meals with the family, ran in and out of the house, and helped Mike with his chores on the houseboats.

And so, tempting as it was to see more of Julie, his determination to succeed won out. She was only eighteen—there was plenty of time. He nodded to himself. He'd get his degree, then come back and see if the spark was still there.

He turned on the ignition and backed out, casting one last lingering glance at the house. Then he drove off, the softness of her lips a sweet memory.

"Hi, Mom. What are you doing out here?" Nick's voice brought Julie back to the present.

"I was just sitting here thinking about the old days."

Nick groaned. "You mean when you had to walk through snowdrifts two feet deep to get to school? Uphill? Both ways?" He stood with his hands on his hips.

Julie laughed. "Yeah, something like that."

He edged closer to her chair. "So was that man a friend of yours too?"

As usual, Nick was being cautious. She couldn't blame him, not after the way his father had treated him. "Not really. When you're in high school, anyone a couple of years ahead is in another world. But he spent a lot of time around our house with your Uncle Mike, so he was like one of the family."

"Oh." Nick absorbed the information. "He seems like a nice guy."

Julie brushed a finger against her lips. "Yeah, he is." She jumped up and headed into the house. "Let's lock up and go to bed. You can read for a while if you like, but I have to get up early."

"Okay." Nick checked the locks on the back door and grabbed a few cookies. He was heavily into science fiction, and she supposed he would be reading well into the night.

Julie watched him fondly, grateful once again that he had turned out so well. *Time for another haircut,* she realized, noticing the hair curling at his collar. His dark hair and eyes were much like his father's, but fortunately, those seemed to be the only traits he had inherited from Brent.

She'd trained herself never to fall asleep with thoughts of Brent in her head. That wouldn't be hard tonight, with Quentin front and center in her mind. She wondered idly how he'd acquired a tan so early in the season—especially since he worked in an office. *I'll ask him the next time I see him,* she thought as she turned out the bedside light, confident that there would be a next time.

"You've got to be kidding!" Maggie's earrings bounced against her neck as she swung her head around. "Quentin Callahan is back in town? How does he look?" She held up her hands, palms out. "No. Wait. Don't tell me." She grabbed the plastic letter opener from her desk and held it to her throat. "If you tell me he's fat and bald I'll slit my throat."

Julie poured herself a cup of coffee and shook in a pack of sugar. "Do you want a refill, Mags?"

Maggie tossed down the letter opener, clearly disappointed

that her theatrics hadn't prompted a response. "Stop toying with me, Julie. What does he look like?"

Julie wandered over to the expanse of windows and stopped. "See for yourself," she said, surprised that her voice sounded so natural. "He's down there." She gestured toward the dock.

Maggie jumped up from her chair and raced to the window. "Oh, my God." Her hand flew to her throat and she turned to her friend, eyes wide. "He's even more gorgeous than before, if that's possible."

Julie tilted her head, watching as Quentin shook hands with Carl. A maintenance cart stood on the dock and Carl gestured back and forth between it and the houseboat. Quentin nodded and they continued talking.

Maggie turned to Julie. "Is he married? What did he say about . . ." She peered at her friend. "Earth to Julie. Come in, please."

Julie was scarcely aware of her friend chattering in the background. Quentin wore a dark blue golf shirt over khaki shorts. *He looks right at home*, she thought, her gaze lingering on muscular legs that ended in sneakers worn with no socks. The two men walked toward the secure area at the end of the dock that housed the fuel and the fuel pump.

Maggie inserted herself between Julie and the window. "I don't believe it," she said, hands on her hips. "You're interested in him already."

"I am not!" Julie's voice was indignant. She frowned at her friend, then moved to the side, just to keep an eye on things. "I'm only trying to figure out what he's doing here, that's all."

"Yeah, right, and I'm the Easter bunny."

"Well, I am." Julie's comeback sounded feeble, even to her own ears.

Maggie took one last look and went back to her desk. "You'd better get down there and see what he's up to, then."

Julie needed no further prompting and ran down the stairs, making her way to the ramp that led onto the dock. The two men were heading back up the dock, and Carl stopped at one of the houseboats, running his finger down the checklist that was taped to the back window.

Quentin spotted her and grinned. "Hi, Boss Lady. I hear you've already put in a couple of hours this morning."

His grin was infectious, and Julie smiled back. "I told you I had to get up early, and nobody calls me Boss Lady around here."

"That's sort of what I came to see you about." He looked around at the houseboats lined up along the dock. "I've decided what I want to do with my month off. I'd like to work for you until you get your staffing situation stabilized."

"You're kidding, right?" She looked from Quentin to Carl. "I can't afford to hire you." Her mind raced. The thought of having him around was definitely appealing, disturbing as his presence might be.

"Come on, Jules. You know I don't expect to be paid." He lifted a hand, as though to touch her, then dropped it to his side. "You'd be doing me a favor. I'm at loose ends, and this place is like a second home to me. You've made a few changes in the way you do things, but the same basic rules still apply. Mike and I did quite a bit of work for your dad our last couple of years in school, if you can remember that far back." His eyes teased her.

"I'm not senile quite yet," she retorted, biting her lip. His offer was tempting, but she had never allowed anyone to work for free, not even the young kids who wanted work experience.

She narrowed her eyes. "I suppose you've been talking to Carl about this."

"Of course. There wouldn't be any point in asking you if he didn't want me around. After all, he'll still be here when I'm long gone."

Julie turned away, shaken by his remark. Of course he'd be leaving when his free time ran out! How had she deluded herself so quickly into thinking that he'd returned for good? She turned back to him and gestured to a large unit that was ready for departure. "Let's talk in here," she said with a grim smile, stepping around a spare propane tank and entering the cabin of the houseboat. She sat at the dining nook and indicated the seat across from her.

"I'm tempted by your offer," she began. "I won't deny that. You already know we could use more help." She glanced around the interior of the cabin as she spoke, finding it spotless. "But I want to make something clear from the outset."

He nodded, eyes fixed on her face.

"You rescued me once, Quentin." Her expression softened. "And I appreciated that more than you know. But I'm not a kid anymore, and I don't need rescuing." Her chin came up a notch and she looked at him steadily. "I've been running this business on my own for a good many years now. It hasn't always been easy, but I love it and I'm willing to sacrifice a lot to keep it going." She blinked rapidly. "I guess what I'm saying is that I'm not the same person anymore. My divorce changed me."

He opened his mouth to speak and she fluttered her fingers, indicating that she wasn't finished. "This is painful to talk about, but you might as well know the whole story. Brent took advantage of me, and when I finally woke up to what was going on, I promised myself that nobody would ever do that to me again. That naïve young girl you rescued all those years ago is gone." She gave him a sad half-smile. "You might even discover that you don't like me very much."

His eyes darkened and he waited several moments before he spoke. "You're not really suggesting that I would take advantage of you, are you?"

Too late, Julie realized that her words had angered him. She shook her head back and forth, but he ignored her and continued talking.

"And as to whether or not I'll come to dislike you, that remains to be seen, but I don't think it's very likely."

Julie chose her words carefully. "I didn't mean to offend you, Quentin. It's just that . . . well, I've become pretty independent since the divorce, and I suppose I find it hard to trust people until they prove themselves." She willed him to understand.

He nodded soberly. "Fair enough. So what do you say? Is it a deal?"

"All right, but I have to give you something in return. What will it be?"

He stood up and walked out onto the rear deck. "Carl says you rarely rent the six-sleepers anymore. Let me stay in one and I'll work my little heart out for you." He pointed to one of the older boats at the end of the dock. "I'd be quite content to call that my home away from home. How's that for a deal?" His eyes challenged her to refuse.

She held out her hand. "It's a deal. Welcome aboard."

He held her hand for a moment longer than necessary and she felt herself being drawn irresistibly toward him.

For one irrational moment she wondered if she would regret inviting Quentin Callahan into her life.

"You won't be sorry, Julie." Had he read her thoughts? "I promise you."

She nodded, not trusting herself to speak. A group of renters rattled down the deck behind a heavily laden ATV, and she found her voice. "Come on up to the office and get the key. You can say hello to Maggie."

Chapter Four

You've gotta be out of your cotton-picking mind." Maggie turned on Julie as soon as Quentin left the office to go back down toward the dock. "How are you going to focus on business with that gorgeous man around here for the next month?"

Julie raised an eyebrow and gave a defiant toss of her head. "No problem, Mags. I'll just remind myself every day that he's outta here in four weeks. That should make it easy."

Maggie tapped her chest several times. "It's me you're talking to, Julie, and I'm not buying it." She sat down on the edge of her desk, all pretense of levity gone. "Listen, I don't want to see you get hurt . . . okay?"

Julie fought back tears. "I understand, Maggie. I really do, but I'll be all right." She put on her professional smile and went out to greet a family group that had just arrived.

Maggie looked after her. "I hope so, my friend. I really hope so."

* * *

Julie worked steadily for the rest of the day, keenly aware of Quentin's presence. He seemed to be everywhere, assisting new arrivals with their supplies, and fueling and servicing the returning boats. There was no indication that he harbored any resentment over her little speech, and as the day wore on she began to relax, exchanging smiles with him when they passed each other on the dock. Her eyes kept seeking him out, and she couldn't help but wonder if Maggie's words would prove prophetic. But on the positive side, he seemed content to take direction from Carl, and he handled the customers with aplomb. At one point she noticed him assisting an elderly woman down the ramp, his head lowered to catch her words as she chatted happily about her grandchildren.

The last rental departed around four in the afternoon, and Carl accompanied Julie to the office to review the next day's requirements.

"I wish we had more large units," announced Maggie as they walked in the door. "I had to turn down two rentals today because they wanted more space."

Julie sighed. It was difficult to keep up with the demands for bigger and more luxurious houseboats. In the beginning, a waterslide had been enough to thrill a family of renters, but nowadays they expected hot tubs, satellite television, sun canopies, and on the largest units, standard equipment included not one but two full-sized barbecues. But now, when she could afford to order larger houseboats, she didn't have enough frontage to accommodate the additional length of the larger boats. As she absorbed Maggie's comment, a twenty-two-sleeper from Apex Houseboats maneuvered out, and she wished once more that there was some way she could build another dock.

"I'll have to give it serious consideration when we're halfway through the season," she said with a shrug. "I'm glad you talked me into that program that tracks how many rental nights we sell for each size of boat."

"Yeah, and how many bookings we turn down," Maggie murmured. Her friend's flamboyant clothing and hairstyles masked a keen business mind, and Julie nodded absently, her gaze returning to the dock.

Quentin disappeared inside a houseboat, carrying an oil change kit. Julie turned to Carl. "Quentin looked busy all day. I hope he was some help to you."

Her maintenance supervisor removed his cap and ran a hand across his rapidly balding head. "Best day I've had for a long time, Julie. He's not afraid to think for himself, and that makes it easy to work together. A couple more days and he won't need any direction at all, you wait and see." He picked up a printout from Maggie and they discussed the boat assignments for tomorrow.

Julie stared out the window, lost in thought. She'd surprised herself, the way the words had come tumbling out earlier today. It was true that her divorce had changed her, but she'd never articulated it before, and as the day wore on she'd begun to question herself. The barriers she'd erected around her heart had protected her and had given her time to heal. But now, in the face of her undeniable attraction to Quentin, she'd been forced to take out her feelings and examine them more closely. And in so doing, she'd acknowledged that living without love was a waste.

She shook her head and turned away from the window, joining Maggie and Carl for the daily operations meeting.

* * *

The sun was low in the sky by the time Quentin checked out of the motel and returned to SunBird. He unpacked his suitcase and hung his clothes in the small wardrobe. He had chosen the largest bedroom for himself, opening the windows to take advantage of the evening breeze. Then he slipped into the shower and adjusted the taps, enjoying the hot water beating down on his tired muscles. *Serves you right for being such a slug*, he told himself. His sailboat had remained tied up all winter, and his short diving holiday in Belize hadn't been particularly physical. A month of hard work would do him good.

He rotated his neck as the water beat down, and a vision of Julie in her shorts and SunBird T-shirt popped into his mind. He liked her current hairdo, and his fingers curled involuntarily as he imagined running them through the mass of blonde hair that framed her face.

"Don't kid yourself, Callahan," he murmured to himself. "After all, she made it clear this afternoon that she's not the same kid you remember." He grabbed a towel. "So back off and do your job."

Within minutes, he pulled on fresh clothes and drove to the grocery store, where he bought enough provisions for the next week. He did not intend to deny himself the pleasure of good food while he was here. Satisfied that he had purchased everything on his mental list, he headed back to his temporary home, whistling softly as he methodically stowed his purchases.

The evening was too pleasant to stay inside. Quentin sauntered down the dock with a deck chair in one hand and a bottle of water in the other. He waved to a young couple in a ski boat heading out onto the lake, and settled himself into the chair. The gentle slap of waves on the bottom of the dock was a familiar sound, and as the ripples from the passing boats subsided, the reflections of the trees on the far bank were mirror images in the still water.

It was time to think about why he had come to Sicamous, and how he would extricate himself from what had rapidly become an untenable situation. He closed his eyes, thinking back to his most recent meeting with Parker Henderson, CEO of Delahunt Holdings, his largest customer.

"We're just not getting anywhere with these people." Henderson tossed a file across his massive desk, clearly frustrated. "They're operating a houseboat business with aging equipment that's getting older every year, and they won't even discuss an offer."

Quentin tried not to react visibly at the mention of houseboats. There was really only one place in British Columbia where houseboat rentals were big business. He reached across the desk and picked up the file.

Report on the Acquisition of SunBird Charters took up less than one page and indicated the reluctance of the present owner to enter into negotiations on the sale of either the business or the land.

"This seems rather straightforward," he said blandly. "If they don't want to sell, there's not much we can do about it." He had been surprised as well as pleased to see that Julie was the legal owner of the business. He suppressed a smile and returned the file to the desk.

"We won't take no for an answer on this, Callahan. There has to be some way we can get our hands on that property." Henderson chuckled mirthlessly. "We've tried everything to make them reconsider, but that woman is obstinate. If something doesn't happen soon, we'll start a price war. We can hold out a lot longer than they can."

Quentin's jaw tightened but he managed to maintain a neutral expression. A price war would hurt all the companies, not just Julie's. And it would create the inevitable ripple effect throughout the small community. But he shouldn't have been surprised, because this wasn't the first time he'd witnessed Delahunt's predatory tactics.

"I can understand your frustration, but nosing around isn't my area of expertise. I'm more of an analyst, a number cruncher."

"I know that." The CEO flicked his pen back and forth on the desk in an annoying staccato. "But you've always been our go-to guy when we're in a jam. We'd like you to look into it and give us your recommendations."

Quentin's brow furrowed. "I wasn't even aware before today that your holdings included a houseboat rental company. That being said, why do you need another one?"

Henderson tossed down his pen. "We don't. We need their land. They're beside us on that incredibly valuable strip of land that runs along Sicamous Narrows."

"Okay." Quentin drew the word out. "But if you buy their company, they'll expect a good price for their assets, and their goodwill. Why don't you simply buy a larger piece of property? Wouldn't that be more cost effective in the long run?" He picked up the file again but didn't open it. "I'm just thinking off the top of my head here."

The other man shot him a scathing look and Quentin was reminded of how much he disliked him. Too bad Delahunt Holdings was his biggest customer. "We don't pay you to think off the top of your head. We pay you for your analytical skills." He leaned back in his chair. "But to answer your question, we've considered that already, and there's nothing available. People up there are crafty, let me tell you. There's a perfect piece of land about half a mile further up the Narrows, but we can't even find out who owns it." He shook his head in reluctant admiration. "Someone has managed to hide their ownership very skillfully."

Quentin's mind raced. Surely there was some way he could deter Delahunt from pressuring Julie. "Why don't you approach these people at the end of the season? Maybe they'll be more receptive then."

"No way. We want action on this right away. We hired some of their people recently and they reported that SunBird is almost completely booked for the season. They won't be in any mood to sell after a successful summer."

"You're probably right, but I don't see that there's much I can do for you here." Quentin replaced the file and picked up his briefcase, anxious to escape. The man across the desk turned his stomach.

"Then I'll have to send Kurt Walker. Trouble is, he's such a barracuda. I thought you'd be smoother, that's all."

Quentin stopped and lowered his briefcase onto the adjoining chair. Walker's tactics were decidedly unpleasant. The choice was clear. Either he could go himself, and risk Julie's anger if she found out his reason for being there, or Delahunt would unleash Kurt Walker on her. The decision was simple, and he had a month off, with no plans.

He forced a conciliatory smile. "You're right. Walker *is* a barracuda, and I daresay a lighter touch is what's needed on this one. What's your time frame for a decision?"

"We'll give it a month. See what you can dig up and find the crack in the dike." The CEO hunched forward, a predator ready to strike. "We want this one, Callahan."

Quentin had never forgotten the night of Julie's graduation, or her response when he kissed her goodnight. Her innocence had made it even sweeter, and he often wondered if she even remembered it. He took a drink of water, eyes unseeing as he stared into the water, pondering the dilemma he now faced. He had come to Sicamous to try to protect her from Delahunt. It was ironic, really. Not only did she not want protection, but she was determined that no man would take advantage of her again.

His thoughts wandered back to that day ten years ago when he'd read about her engagement in the local paper. He'd thought about her often, but in his mind she'd stayed the same, and he was unprepared for the sharp jab of pain when he read the announcement. For one fleeting moment he'd considered making a quick trip back to Sicamous, to see if anything remained of the spark that had ignited on that night.

But he'd managed to rein himself in. After all, no promises had been made—on either side. So he'd done the only thing he could and plunged back into his studies, hoping that she'd found a great guy who would make her happy.

He couldn't help but wonder now what her husband had done to make her so cautious, but instinct told him that in time she would confide in him. In the meantime, if she ever found out why he was here, she would . . . To his surprise, he found that he couldn't even imagine her reaction.

What he hadn't planned on was his own response to seeing her again. Working beside her would be sweet agony, but he reminded himself of his reason for being there. He couldn't foresee what would happen a month down the road, but for now he was content to work at her side and watch over her. Last week, in the offices of Delahunt Holdings, he'd started to formulate the beginnings of a plan he hoped would make them back off. He drained the water bottle, considering how best to proceed. If he timed everything right, it might work. It just might work.

"They're giving us the lists tonight." Nick placed his dinner plate and cutlery in the dishwasher. "So we'll know everything we need for camp. It's not a regular meeting, so I should be home early."

"I miss you already. Come here and give me a hug." Julie was at the sink.

Nick rolled his eyes. "Come on, Mom. Don't you think I'm getting a bit big for hugs?"

Julie laughed and rumpled his hair. "Never, my boy. Go on, now, and I'll see you later."

She watched as he rode off on his bike. Camp would be good for him, although the house would be quiet while he was gone.

She wandered into the spacious living room, automatically plumping the cushions on the couch. Directly over the office, it offered the same view of the marina. This was a peaceful time of day, and like she did every evening at this time, she counted the number of units in their slips. As she did, her eyes were drawn to the solitary figure seated at the end of the main dock. Quentin was leaning back in a deck chair, hands clasped behind his head. He appeared deep in thought.

She hesitated for only a moment, then picked up a

sweater and ran down the double flight of stairs to the lawn. Her bare feet allowed her to move in silence until a loose board announced her presence. He unhooked his hands and turned slowly, his eyes pulling her closer.

"Hello, Jules." Quentin stood up and moved to the nearest houseboat, lifting a folded deck chair over the back railing. He placed it beside his chair and motioned for her to sit down. "May I offer you something to drink?" He picked up the empty water bottle. "I was about to graduate to Pellegrino."

"No, thanks. I just finished dinner."

He nodded, and his eyes moved back to the water.

Julie sat down and looked at him curiously. He seemed quiet tonight, as though he had something on his mind. "How was your day?" she asked. "Were you bored with what you were doing?"

"No, not at all." He smiled, and his face was transformed. "As a matter of fact, I should thank you for letting me hang out here. It's exactly what I need to help me decide what's next in my life."

Julie inhaled sharply. His smile made her stomach flutter and she silently chided herself. She was acting irrational, that's all there was to it. She shifted in her chair, wondering yet again if she'd made a mistake by agreeing to let him stay on *Chickadee*. He'd awakened something in her, and she wasn't sure if she was ready. Or was she?

"I didn't expect this to be happening to me right now." Quentin's voice brought her out of her reverie. It was low— tentative almost—nothing like the way he usually spoke. "I worked hard to get where I am and yet now, all of a sudden, I don't know which way to turn." He shot a sideways look in her direction. "I have to make an important decision soon . . . one that could change the rest of my life."

It was unsettling to see him like this. Quentin had always known where he was going, what he wanted out of life. "Can I help?" she asked.

He reached out and touched her arm. The contact was brief yet electric. "Thanks, Julie, but this is something I have to figure out for myself."

"Maybe I *will* have something to drink," she said abruptly. "Do you have any orange Pellegrino?"

"Coming right up." He leaped up and strode across the dock, returning a moment later with two bottles and one glass. He poured her drink and handed it to her with a small bow. She held up the glass, watching the bubbles race to the surface.

Once seated, he leaned forward, elbows on his knees. "Now you're the thoughtful one."

She glanced at him, acknowledging his words, then pulled the sweater around her shoulders. "I can relate to how you're feeling," she said after a moment. "I should have divorced Brent much sooner, but I wanted to make the marriage work. Not for myself so much, but I had it in my head that I didn't want to deprive Nick of a father." She frowned, thinking back to those unhappy times.

"I'd read about your wedding in the local newspaper, but I didn't hear about your divorce until I ran into Sharon Cooke in Vancouver." His eyes softened. "I'm sorry, Julie."

She nodded and looked off into the distance. "You know, things were fine for the first couple of years. He worked down at the sawmill and I worked here with Mom and Dad. It was a normal marriage, I think. And then Nick came along and I thought my life was complete." She pressed the cool glass against her forehead.

"When it was all over, I could have kicked myself for not recognizing the signs sooner, but maybe I just didn't want to see it. I don't know." She paused. "He'd always gambled, you know, but then that casino opened in Vernon and it seemed to take over his life. By then, Mom and Dad had retired and I was running the business. He saw it as his own private source of funding. I found out later that the few times I confronted him he took it out on Nicky." Her fingers tightened around the glass. "He couldn't turn on me, of course, because I was the sucker who kept bailing him out. But then one day I came home and found him yelling at Nick. He had his hand raised, and I swear he was going to hit him." Her voice was clogged with emotion. "I knew that was it. He told me to go to hell and I was at the lawyer's office the next day."

"Where is he now?"

"I don't know, and I honestly don't care. He doesn't pay any child support, and that's fine with me. The worst part was the guilt I felt for subjecting Nicky to all that, but when I saw the way he bloomed after Brent was gone, we both put it behind us." She took a drink and set her glass down on the deck. "It was quite a blow to my self-esteem when he finally told me I was nothing more to him than a bankroll."

Quentin placed his hand over hers. "He didn't deserve you, Julie."

He withdrew his hand and she almost reached for him, to feel the warmth of his flesh against hers, to feel the magic that sparked between them every time they touched. She had never admitted it to anyone, but Brent's touch—even in the good times—had never thrilled her. He'd never measured up against that one brief interlude with Quentin Callahan. She looked at him curiously, wondering what it would be like to be this man's woman. Whoa there! Time to change the subject.

"Have you been getting the local newspaper, then? You said you read about my wedding."

"I've had a subscription ever since I moved away." He laughed. "I've read about businesses opening and closing, new mayors being elected, and I've followed the swings in the real estate market." He tilted his bottle and seemed surprised to find it empty. "Although with real estate, it's been mostly an upswing. Anyway, it's different to be here, to see it in person."

His voice softened. "Like seeing you, Julie. Funny how we always remember people as they were the last time we saw them. I kept remembering you the way you looked that night."

She couldn't look at him. "You said I looked beautiful. You made me feel special, and I always remembered that. Thank you."

"It was the truth." He leaned back in the chair and studied her. "And now you're even lovelier. Maturity sits well on you, Jules."

She was suddenly uncomfortable, twisting the arms of her sweater in her lap. If he kept talking like that, she really would fall for him, but she couldn't afford to do that. She couldn't bear the heartbreak that would most certainly follow when he went back to the coast. She had to push him away before it was too late.

"My goodness," she said, hoping he couldn't see the pulse pounding at her throat. "Are you making a pass at the boss?"

"Why, no, ma'am. I'm just stating the facts as I see them." His gaze devoured her lazily. "And I like what I see."

An unaccustomed blush crept up her neck and into her face. What was happening to her? She jumped up and laughed nervously. "Nicky should be getting home any minute now. He's excited because he's off to camp with the Cub Scouts next week." She started walking back up the dock, and he caught up with her in a few strides.

"Do they still go to that lake up in the hills behind Salmon Arm?"

"Yes. This will be his third year up there. He loves it."

"You've done a great job with him, Julie." He paused outside *Chickadee*. "This is me."

She looked up at him. "Did you get the duvet I sent down for you this afternoon?"

"Did you send that? Thanks. It'll keep me cozy in bed on these cool nights."

"Hmm." They gazed into each other's eyes and Julie was the first to look away. "I'd better get going." She smiled weakly, wishing he would ask her to stay. But that would only lead to complications, and besides, Nicky would be home shortly.

"See you in the morning, then." He stepped onto the deck of the small houseboat. "Carl tells me we should have a busy day tomorrow."

"Huh? Oh, that's right." Reality brought her crashing back to earth, and she backed away. "Good night, Quentin. Thanks for the drink." She turned and headed up the ramp.

His dimple flashed and he raised his hand in a silent salute as she climbed the stairs. "Any time, sweet lady," he said softly. "Any time at all."

Nick wasn't home, and Julie stood in the darkened living room, staring out over the marina. Blue-grey light flickered from the television in *Chickadee,* and she could see Quentin's shadow moving back and forth as he prepared his evening meal. His presence was complicating her life, but she simply didn't care. Tomorrow couldn't arrive soon enough.

Chapter Five

Julie awoke, and her heart started to beat a little faster. Had she dreamed about Quentin again last night? She reached back into her mind, but there were no lingering dream-memories. She had never told anyone—certainly not Maggie—about the number of times she'd relived that long-ago night in her sleep. It was foolish—it really was—and she knew it. But the dreams left her feeling protected . . . cherished . . . and, in her dream, loved.

She looked out her window, where the aspens quivered with the morning breeze. It was her favorite time of day, her problem-solving time.

She jumped out of bed and padded to the shower. So, what was she going to do about Quentin? She stuck her hand under the water, waiting for it to warm up. The plumbing rattled a bit but she scarcely heard it.

She couldn't deny that Quentin had always been a factor in her life. For the first few months after their encounter on her graduation night she eagerly checked the mail every day, hoping that he might have written. But as summer turned into fall she started to accept that she wasn't going to hear from him. She clung to the faint hope that he would come home for Christmas, but he didn't show up, which was just as well, because his father had been engaged in a drunken brawl and spent the week in jail.

And so, in her own quiet way, she did what she'd always done. She got on with her life, which centered on the houseboat company. She worked most days, taking very little time for social activities, and so her friends and family were surprised when she brought Brent home. They were even more surprised when she accepted his proposal.

She stood under the shower, rinsing shampoo from her hair and thinking of the mess she'd made of her life. Well, not completely a mess. She had Nicky, but he was growing up quickly and she was determined not to become a clinging single mother.

She stepped out of the shower, dried off, and stared at herself in the mirror. She saw dark blue eyes, a generous mouth, and hair that was already starting to spring into unruly curls. Not bad. Quentin had said that she was even lovelier than before, but that might be a bit of a stretch. She smiled at herself. He was interested, she was quite sure of it. She ran her fingers through her hair, then leaned into the mirror. Would she *really* be brokenhearted if they had a summertime romance and he want back to Vancouver? Or was that just an excuse? She'd kept her heart protected for so long she'd begun to think of it as something fragile. She gave a soft snort of derision. The truth was, she was a strong, independent woman.

She entered her living room just as the sun crested over the hill, bathing the marina in the fresh light of the summer morning. There was no evidence of the two chairs at the end of the dock. It was as if last night had never happened, but she knew that it hadn't been a dream. She also knew that it was time she opened herself to love. It was time to start living again.

"Good morning, Maggie." Julie did a double take. Her friend was dressed conservatively, in white linen slacks and a tailored black shirt, cinched at the waist with a broad gold belt. Gold hoop earrings completed her ensemble. "I like the outfit. What's up?"

Maggie turned, held up a finger for silence, and Julie noticed the headset. "No, sir, I don't think it was a rat. Are you pulled up at one of the regular beaches that we've marked on the map?" She made a face at Julie, showing her exasperation with the caller on the radiophone. "And did you leave the boarding ramp out last night?" She tapped her pencil on her notepad, where she had written CHIPMUNK in large letters for Julie to see. "Well, sir, that was a chipmunk. They have become accustomed to being fed, and they'll scamper right into your boat looking for food if you leave the ramp out." She nodded in reply to what was being said. "You're very welcome. Enjoy the rest of your charter, sir."

She turned to Julie. "The day wouldn't be complete without a 'rat' sighting. It never ceases to amaze me that some people can't tell the difference between a rat and a chipmunk." She tore off the headset. "Now, what was that you were saying? If it was a compliment, I'm all ears."

"That's what I like about you, Mags. You're so subtle." Julie walked around her friend's desk, viewing her from all angles. "This is a great new look. Have you got a hot date or something?"

"No, but I did meet someone interesting last night. You know that group of fellows who are going out today?" Julie nodded. "Well, they stopped in yesterday to make sure everything was hunky dory, and they asked me out for drinks."

"And you accepted."

"Natch, and we had a good time. They're nice guys who met each other at UBC, and they try to get together every couple of years. Some sort of male bonding thing. Anyway, I want to look my best when they come back today. One of them has real potential. He's from Vancouver, and I wouldn't mind knowing someone down there I could call when I go to the big smoke." She examined her fingernails. "He's a lawyer."

Julie had drifted over to the window and smiled as she caught sight of Quentin.

Maggie looked out to see what had triggered the smile. "Oh, I almost forgot. Palmer—that's his name, by the way—Palmer told me he knows Quentin from somewhere. I guess he spotted him down on the dock yesterday, and he was questioning me about him last night. He says he can't quite recall where he's seen him before, but he'll think about it." Her eyes sparkled, and she tossed her head. "We have a date when he comes back."

Julie chuckled. "You're incorrigible. Are you trolling for husband number three?"

"No way." Maggie shook her head. "Besides, you couldn't manage around here without me."

"You've got that right." She turned a thoughtful eye on her friend. "But even so, I hope you wouldn't let work stand in the way of a possible romance. I hate to sound like one of those saccharine slogans we both hate so much, but life's too short, kiddo."

Maggie pulled back. "Okay, who are you and what have you done with my friend?"

"Talk about corny, overused lines," murmured Julie.

"All right, all right, but that doesn't sound like you, and you know it. Remember last month, when you refused to go out with Larry's friend? I even set it up as a foursome, so you wouldn't feel too much pressure. But would you go? Nooooo." Maggie started to draw little hearts on the scratch pad by her telephone. "I distinctly remember that at one point you said that romance was highly overrated."

Julie turned away. Why had she started this conversation, anyway? When Maggie got on a subject that she felt strongly about, she was like the proverbial dog with a bone. She wouldn't let it go, and Julie knew it.

"Okay, I might have been wrong."

"Sorry, I couldn't hear you. Would you repeat that, please?"

"You heard me." Julie had to laugh. "I said I might have been wrong." She walked over to the coffeepot, playing for time to find the right words. Maggie remained silent.

"I know I've talked a lot about not wanting to get involved, but I was thinking about Nicky this morning."

"Huh? You just lost me."

Julie continued as if Maggie hadn't spoken. "He's growing up so quickly. I'm trying not to be one of those single mothers who pour all their love into their kid. Sometimes I worry that I might smother him . . . you know . . . be too protective. I wanted to give him a hug the other day and he said he was getting too big."

Maggie rolled her eyes. "Come on, Julie. That's only normal."

"Yeah, I suppose so. But it got me thinking. The years

are flying past, and before long he's probably going to want to leave home. I'd hate it, but I'd support him."

"And then you'd be alone," Maggie said quietly.

"Exactly." Julie stared into her coffee. "I know it goes against everything I've been saying since Brent, but I think it's time I learned to trust men again. They're not all like him, I know that, but the walls have been up for so long. . . ." Her voice tapered off.

"This wouldn't have anything to do with the fact that Quentin is back?" Maggie wrinkled her nose. "Nah, it couldn't be that."

"No, of course not." Julie's smile indicated just the opposite. "But it is convenient." She settled behind her desk and switched on her computer. "Since we aren't expecting any arrivals for a few hours I thought I'd order supplies."

"Good idea. Take a look at the sample Christmas cards, would you? I've got the customer list all updated and I could start doing the envelopes in my spare time as soon as they arrive."

Julie was soon absorbed in her work, and the morning flew by. At one point she glanced out the window and was surprised to see Nick down on the dock, talking to Quentin. She smiled as her son took a long-handled brush from Quentin and proceeded to scrub down the deck of a returned boat. Tearing her eyes away from the pair, she turned to find Maggie observing them as well.

"I hope Nicky doesn't get too attached to him." Maggie watched while Quentin trained a hose on the deck Nick had scrubbed. "He's practically a fixture around here already. It's easy to forget that he's not sticking around."

"*I* haven't forgotten." Julie clamped her mouth shut.

"Did I say I was talking about you?" Maggie gave Julie an innocent look, one eyebrow raised. "I don't think so. I distinctly remember mentioning Nicky's name."

"Oh, all right, Mags. You've made your point." Julie's eyes lingered on Quentin and at that moment he threw back his head and laughed at something Nick said. She couldn't recall ever seeing Brent and Nick laughing together like that, and her heart swelled. A returning houseboat pulled up to the end of the dock and Nick ran to catch the lines, turning to Quentin for approval. The look of pride on his face when he received a thumbs-up was a like a precious gift. At that moment, Julie thought that she could bear any amount of heartbreak if it meant happy memories for her son.

She turned away just in time to see her friend wiping a tear from the corner of her eye.

"That does it," said Maggie, dabbing at her eyes. "Don't listen to me, kiddo. He's just too good to pass up. But you already figured that out for yourself, didn't you?"

Julie nodded. "It crossed my mind once or twice." She picked up a paper clip from her desk and absently linked it with another as she spoke. "I've been an emotional cripple for too long, Mags. If I carry on like this, I might as well still be married to Brent. It's time I put aside all the hurt and started living again." Her gaze went back to the scene down on the dock. "And I think Quentin can show me what I've been missing."

"Stop it! You're making me cry." Maggie laughed through her tears. "You've earned some happiness. I hope you find it."

*   *   *

Nick came bounding into the office in the early afternoon. Julie had offered to watch the phones as Maggie showed the party of four men to their rental.

"Quentin's cool," he announced. "He knows lots of neat stuff."

"You see? Adults aren't necessarily boring."

"Right, Mom. Can I go now and meet Tommy and Ryan? We're just going to hang out this afternoon."

"Sure, sweetheart. What time will you be home for dinner?"

"Early, Mom. We have a baseball game tonight, remember?"

"How could I forget? You only reminded me three times in the past couple of days. See you later, then." Nick rode off on his bike, both of his baseball gloves hooked over the handlebars.

"I took two new reservations while you were out and entered them into the computer." Julie showed Maggie her notes. "I didn't see your friends pull out, but I assume they got underway all right."

"Oh yeah." Maggie reclaimed her desk. "That boat has a full quota of testosterone, I can tell you that much. They were like young kids, elbowing each other out of the way, seeing who would take the helm first."

"Did your friend say anything more about Quentin?" Julie was anxious for any nuggets of information.

"No, but he glanced over at him a couple of times."

"Speaking of which, I think I'll wander down to the dock and see if the magic is still alive."

"You *have* changed." Maggie shooed her out the door, then turned to answer the telephone. Quentin was fuelling one of the day's returning boats and looked up as Julie rounded the corner at the end of the dock. "Hi there." He gave her a heart-stopping grin, then turned his attention back to the fuel gauge. "Nick was a real help this morning, but I guess you saw us."

Julie nodded. He looked completely at home on the dock, and she'd been pleased to see from the checklists that both returns had been serviced. The cleaning crew was finishing the first boat and would start on this one as soon as Quentin moved it to the public area.

"Carl and I are going to do some general maintenance checks this afternoon," he said, returning the nozzle to its cradle. "And I hope you don't mind, but I told Nick he could bring his friends back to look around."

"Of course not." They both turned as three boys came thundering down the ramp. "Which is a good thing, because here they are already."

Quentin turned to greet Nick and his two friends. The young visitors puffed up with importance as he solemnly shook their hands, introducing himself. He showed Tommy and Ryan around the dock, taking special care to point out the tasks Nick had performed that morning. Tommy peppered Quentin with questions while Ryan remained silent, his eyes darting from Quentin to Nick, then back again to the older man. When the tour was finished, Quentin offered the boys a soft drink.

"Come on over to *Chickadee*, and you can choose your own poison."

Nick and Tommy bounded off, chattering nonstop, and Quentin followed. The boys selected a soda, then ran up onto the lawn. Ryan hung back, standing off to the side next to one of the pilings. "You too, Ryan," he said gently, and the boy scooted past him and ran up the dock without claiming the offered drink. Quentin shot a puzzled look at Julie, then looked thoughtfully after the young boy, lost in thought.

Carl called down from the top deck of *Osprey*, where he'd been checking the sun canopy. "He's good with the kids, isn't he?" He hiked his head toward Quentin, who had gone to move the twelve-sleeper.

"Yes, he is." Julie's voice softened and she looked after Quentin, unaware that her eyes were glowing. She looked back up at Carl to find him watching her with an odd expression on his face. Or maybe she'd imagined it. Everything was changing so quickly.

Carl nodded his approval and continued his inspection.

Julie caught up with the boys, who were now sprawled under the shade of the weeping willow, passing the drink cans back and forth and seeing who could produce the loudest burp.

"Quentin says he'd like to take us out for hamburgers before our baseball game tonight." Nick's upturned face was eager. "He said we should ask you if that's all right. He invited Tommy and Ryan too."

"I can't go." Tommy's face mirrored his disappointment. "I have to go home and get my uniform and my glove. But I told him thanks, anyway."

"Me too." Ryan's voice was subdued. "My mom's expecting me home soon." He glanced over Julie's shoulder and she turned to see Quentin coming toward them.

"Are you game?" he asked. "Nothing fancy. I thought maybe the same place we went the other night."

"Please, Mom. Can we go? Please?" Nick fidgeted as he waited for a reply.

"Okay," agreed Julie. "It'll save a bit of time if I don't have to cook."

"Your mom and I had buffalo burgers the last time," said Quentin as Nick studied the menu on the chalkboard. "They were good."

"Yuck! I don't want to eat an old buffalo." Nick wrinkled his nose. "I'll have the regular hamburger," he told the amused employee behind the counter. "And fries, please."

The trio settled down at a picnic table on the outdoor deck of the restaurant, Nick chatting excitedly about the upcoming game. Julie relaxed and listened with half an ear, sipping her coffee, content to be a part of what she knew must resemble a happy family group. She had dreamed of times like this when she was first married, but those dreams hadn't materialized.

And now here she was with Quentin, who encouraged Nick with questions about the team and their exploits. She gave herself a mental shake. It would be too easy to become comfortable with the notion of the three of them as a family group. She'd tried to talk to Nick when his father left, and although he'd never said much, she knew that Brent's desertion must have hurt him. And now Quentin had come into their lives and she already knew that he was leaving. She didn't want to subject her son to heartbreak all over again. She looked up to find Quentin watching her. His eyes were serious, almost as if he could read her thoughts.

Nick ran out of steam just as the hamburgers were delivered. "This is great," he mumbled after the first enormous bite.

"You know the rules," Julie admonished.

Nick swallowed. "Yeah, no talking with my mouth full."

He dived back in and cleaned up his plate in what must have been record time.

"You guys are quiet," he said, draining his soda. "They should have one of those old-fashioned jukeboxes around here."

"Wait just a minute, young man." Quentin grinned. "Your mother and I are old enough to remember when there were jukeboxes everywhere, and we don't consider ourselves old-fashioned."

"Yeah, I know," said Nick. "Every time we go to the diner she looks for a song by some old guy. Old King Cole or something."

Julie knew she was blushing, and was unable to meet Quentin's gaze.

"You mean Nat King Cole," he said, a smile lighting his eyes. "He sang one of the most beautiful love songs ever written, called 'When I Fall In Love.'"

Nick looked from Quentin to his mother, eyes wide. "Hey, that's the one Mom always plays. You guys really are old-fashioned." He jumped up from the bench and ran to the railing as a houseboat glided past.

Julie kept her eyes on her plate, mortified by Nick's revelation.

"You remembered." Quentin reached across the table and took her hand. "Look at me, Julie," he whispered. "I want to see your eyes when you tell me that you haven't forgotten."

She raised her head slowly, and the look on his face made her breath catch in her throat. The years fell away, and they were once more sitting in the diner, listening to the beguiling voice of Nat King Cole sing about love.

"I never forgot," she said simply, a soft smile playing

around her lips. "For the longest time, I judged everyone against you, against my memories of you, and every time I heard that song my knees would go weak." Her eyes held his, no longer hiding her feelings. "It was a wonderful memory, and I cherished it for many years."

"Thank you for saying that."

"Why?"

"Because I often wondered if you even remembered me. You looked so beautiful that night." He smiled in remembrance. "You glowed. There's no other way to put it."

She smiled, suddenly shy. "I was an impressionable teenager who had just lost her heart to her rescuer. I thought I was in love with you that night."

Quentin looked down at her hand in his and his voice was heavy with emotion when he spoke. "Do you think—"

Julie groaned inwardly as Nick came bouncing back to the table. "Come on, we're going to be late." He looked at his mother's plate. "No dessert for you, Mom. You didn't even eat half your food."

"We'll see about that." She made an effort to sound bright. "I was thinking we could go for ice cream after the game. My treat." She stepped away from the table. "All right, let's go."

At the ballpark, Nick ran ahead to join his teammates while Julie and Quentin found a spot in the small viewing stands. Nick had brought both of his gloves, and he slipped one to Ryan as they gathered around their coach.

As the game got under way Quentin scanned the crowd. "Are Ryan's parents here?" he asked under his breath.

Julie looked around and shook her head. "Come to think of it, I don't believe I've ever seen them at a game." She jumped up and cheered as Nick snagged a ground ball from his position at third base and fired it at second base. "Why do you ask?" She sat back down and rubbed her arms.

"Oh, nothing. I'm just trying to put faces to the names. Are you cold? Seems like I'm always warming you up. Hold on a sec and I'll get my jacket from the car."

He returned a moment later and slipped his jacket over her shoulders, then climbed to the bench above her and cradled her between his legs. "Lean back on me and you'll be out of the wind."

Julie sighed and leaned back, resting her elbows on his knees. "That's better," she murmured, savoring the sensation of being cared for. He held her lightly through the rest of the ball game, cheering loudly for Nick's team. Julie couldn't remember the last time she'd enjoyed a game this much.

Nick's spirits were high after the game, even though his team lost by one run. "It was better than before," he said cheerfully. "They really creamed us last time we played them."

"So, how about it? Would you and your friends like to go for ice cream?" The breeze had turned cool, and Julie slid her arms into the sleeves of Quentin's jacket. "Why I ever suggested ice cream is beyond me," she murmured, "but a promise is a promise."

Ryan stared at the ground, kicking at a patch of grass with a scuffed sneaker.

"Can you come with us?" asked Julie.

The boy looked up, and she was struck by the haunted yet hopeful expression in his eyes. "Okay," he said after a moment. He gave her a tentative smile.

"We'll drive you home afterward." Quentin rested his hand on the boy's shoulder. Dark eyes looked at him solemnly, and Ryan nodded.

They sat at the picnic tables on the diner patio, thoughtfully keeping the boisterous boys outside, away from the other diners.

"Hey, this is the place with the jukeboxes," said Nick as he dug for the last of the chocolate syrup in the bottom of his sundae.

"Yeah, we know," said Quentin, looking at Julie with a slow smile. "We've been here before."

She met his gaze steadily, seeing the promise of new beginnings.

Chapter Six

Mike!" Julie was delighted to hear her brother's voice on the phone. "How are you?"

"We're fine, sis. If this great weather keeps up, we thought we'd head down your way for a bit of a holiday."

She walked to the window. A group of customers milled about on the dock, loading supplies into their houseboat. "That's fantastic. I was just telling Quentin the other day that I don't see you often enough."

"Quentin Callahan? You're kidding. What's that old dog doing down there?"

Julie chuckled. "This is going to sound crazy, but he's helping out here at the marina. He says he needed a break from his consulting business."

"You're right, that does sound crazy. But hey, whatever turns you on, I guess."

Julie blushed as she watched Quentin pointing out the features of the houseboat, his long legs even more tanned than before. She wondered what her brother would think if he knew what was turning *her* on these days.

"When will you be arriving?"

"Sorry, I can't give you an exact date, but probably in three or four days. We're going to stop and visit Sharon's parents on the way and then just mosey on down. Is that all right with you?"

"Sure, no problem." She paused. "It'll be good to see you again, Mike."

"You too, Jules. And tell Callahan I want a complete update when I get there."

"Will do."

Julie hung up and turned to Maggie. "I guess you heard. Mike and his family are arriving some time in the next week or so. You know, I think I'll phone Mom and Dad right now and ask if they want to come for a visit at the same time. We could have a real family reunion."

Julie smiled as she hung up the phone after speaking to her mother. "It couldn't have worked out better. They're going to the Calgary Stampede, so they'll stop here on the way and visit with Mike."

The conversation was interrupted by the arrival of another family group, and Julie showed the husband the ATVs and carts, while the wife completed the paperwork with Maggie. Once they were organized, she accompanied them onto the dock, and turned them over to Carl for indoctrination.

Quentin looked down at her as he emptied the hot tub on the roof of the largest unit. "Did you get Nick settled down last night?"

He managed to make the question sound intimate, and she smiled up at him, shading her eyes from the sun. "Eventually," she replied. "Although he bounced around for quite a while."

"Pass up that hose, would you?" He reached down, strong

fingers curling around the hose, and her eyes were drawn to the golden hair on his forearms. Their fingers touched briefly, and she looked away, wondering if he could see the longing in her eyes.

"Hey," she said breathlessly, pretending to look at the check sheet. "Mike called this morning. He's bringing his family down sometime in the next week."

Quentin's smile broadened. "That's great. We have a lot of catching up to do."

"He said the same thing, and he said to warn you that he expects a full report."

"Speaking of family"—his voice turned serious—"I'm going to visit my dad tonight."

"That's great. Does he know you're coming?"

"They said they'd let him know. He wasn't available when I called, but they suggested that I come down and have dinner with him in the dining room." His eyes clouded with uncertainty, and Julie felt a sudden surge of anger toward the man who had wallowed in sorrow and neglected his only son.

"I'm glad you're going. It'll be fine, I'm sure."

"If it's not too late, I'll stop by the house and tell you about it when I get back." He gave a short, terse laugh. "I don't mind admitting that I'm a bit apprehensive about this."

"Don't worry about how late it is. I'll be waiting."

"Thanks, Julie." His eyes softened, and he looked almost like his old self again. "See you later."

Quentin tried to gather his thoughts as he drove toward the seniors' complex in Vernon. His memories of his mother were vague. She had been kind, gentle, and affectionate, but he'd been too young to appreciate her as a person. She was "his mom"—always there, always proud of his accomplishments. That is, until the last year, when her illness had been all consuming. The brightness had gone out of the home, and out of his life.

After her death, his father had become a different person. Never openly affectionate, he rarely spoke to his son, except to berate him—often for imagined transgressions. Threats of a beating came frequently, and Quentin became adept at keeping out of range of his father's hands.

His own hands gripped the steering wheel so tightly they ached, and he forced himself to relax. In retrospect, it was a wonder that his father had kept his job. But he did, up until his retirement a few years ago. Quentin frowned. The move to the retirement home had been unexpected, and Quentin wasn't sure what he'd find.

Quentin glanced around the cheerful reception area, which led into a lounge where a woman with a hunched back and snowy white curls was playing the piano. She was surprisingly good. Several other residents listened, walkers pushed off to the side, and in a corner two feeble-looking older gentlemen braced themselves against a billiards table, cue sticks in hand.

"I'm here to see Mr. Callahan, please." He smiled at the receptionist. She wore a bright smock and a cheerful expression.

"You're his son?" Her eyes widened briefly. "Yes, we've been expecting you." She picked up a telephone. "Mrs. Peters would like to have a word with you first, if you don't mind."

He was ushered into an office bearing the title of "Manager" on the door, and a middle-aged woman rose to greet him.

"I'm Roma Peters," the woman said, extending her hand. "It's a pleasure to meet you."

Quentin remained standing.

"Please, sit down."

He did as requested.

"Before you visit with your father I wanted to have a word." She shot him a quick, curious look. "I understand that you haven't seen him for some years."

He wasn't sure what she was getting at, but the statement was true. "That's right."

"That remark was not intended as a criticism, Mr. Callahan." She pushed some papers around on her desk. "It's just that I believe you'll find your father has changed a great deal since you last saw him."

Quentin looked at her steadily. "I expected that, but to be frank, I've been wondering what he's doing here. He's a good deal younger than most of your residents, being sixty-nine."

The manager returned his gaze. "While it's true that he's younger than most of the other residents, I think you'll find that his health has deteriorated quite a bit."

"That's not surprising, Mrs. Peters. My father started drinking heavily after my mother died. Alcohol does terrible things to the body."

"Yes." She pursed her lips. "Your father's doctor filled me in on his background, but your father doesn't drink anymore, Mr. Callahan. He has Alzheimer's."

He looked at her as though she were speaking a foreign language. "Alzheimer's."

"Yes."

Quentin's thoughts were in disarray, and he looked around, as if the walls of the office would help him to make sense of this startling news. "Is he aware that he has Alzheimer's? Did he check himself in here?"

"I believe that your father and Dr. Austen were more than patient and doctor. I understand that they liked to fish together when your father was younger."

Quentin vaguely remembered something about fishing. "He told you this?"

"Yes, and when your father began to realize that his mind was going, he discussed it with Dr. Austen. He was a great help to your father when it came time to sell his home and move into the facility."

Quentin couldn't meet her eyes. "I should have been there for him."

"You didn't know?"

"I had no idea." He took a deep breath. "Over the years I tried to keep in touch with birthday cards and Christmas cards, but they were never acknowledged. So, about five years ago I came up for a quick visit. He was drinking, but he knew what he was saying when he told me to get out of his house and never come back." He gave her a bleak look. "I did as he asked. I can't help but wonder if I'd persevered, maybe I'd have seen the signs."

"Well, I can assure you of one thing." Mrs. Peters' voice was gentle.

"What's that?"

"Your father would have developed Alzheimer's no matter what."

Quentin absorbed this information, but it didn't lessen the pain. He finally spoke. "Will he know me?"

"Perhaps. It's hard to predict." The manager glanced up at the wall clock and came around from behind her desk. "Would you like to see him now? The residents are going in to lunch, and one of the girls has gone to get him from his room." She gave Quentin a weak smile. "He doesn't have much awareness of time, and he forgets to eat if we don't bring him down for meals. Even then, he eats very little."

Quentin tried to prepare himself, but the sight of his father shuffling down the hallway was a shock. The tall, vigorous man who had been his father had shrunk by several inches. Painfully thin, he held on to the railing along the wall.

"Hello, Dad." Quentin could barely speak.

"Hello." His father paused and looked at him, a puzzled expression in his eyes. "Who are you?"

Quentin's heart thudded in his chest, and he was surprised he could speak. "I'm your son, Quentin."

"Quentin?" For several heartbeats, the fog lifted from his eyes. "Where's your mother? I can't find her anywhere." His gaze skittered around the reception area, and he started to fidget.

The attendant moved, drawing his attention. "Come on, Mr. Callahan. Let's look for her in the dining room."

They were seated at a table for four. The other two residents greeted his father brightly, but he did not acknowledge them. They gave Quentin an encouraging smile, then started in on their soup. His father looked vaguely around the dining room, and pushed away the small bowl of soup that had been placed in front of him.

"Your father doesn't really like soup. I don't know why they keep bringing it to him," volunteered one of the women. The other nodded.

Quentin forced himself to eat a few spoonfuls of soup, watching his father for another spark of recognition.

"He doesn't say much," the first woman said. "But the other day he was telling us about the fishing trips he used to go on. Didn't you, Hugh?"

The meal was the longest of Quentin's life. His father spoke only once, and the words that came out made no sense. Behind his vapid eyes, Quentin sensed fear, as though his father knew what was happening but was helpless to stop it. He ate only a few bites of his main course, but consumed the entire bowl of pudding that was placed before him for dessert.

After lunch, the attendant came to the table. "Would you like to sit in the lounge and listen to the music?"

"No!" His father shook his head, then looked at Quentin, a puzzled look on his face. "Who are you?" he said, as though just noticing him.

"I'm Quentin. I'm your son."

His father peered at him, and for a moment it looked as though he might remember, but he simply shook his head and started to shuffle toward his room, accompanied by the attendant. He didn't look back.

Quentin didn't recall driving the return trip, but he found himself sitting in the SunBird parking lot, staring blankly over the steering wheel. His head was reeling. There were so many questions, he didn't know where to start. In his business life, he was always in control, always analytical, but this uncertainty left him shaken and confused. Getting out of his car, he almost fell, but he caught himself and headed down the lawn to his little houseboat, his gait stiff and irregular. He didn't notice the soothing warmth of the evening air, or the brilliance of the stars in the sky. He slid back the door of the houseboat and stumbled across the small interior to the dining nook, where he lowered himself onto the bench. Propping his elbows onto the table, he lowered his head into his hands.

After dinner, Julie had a quick shower. Nick was spending the night at Tommy's, in a tent at the rear of their property. She smiled, wondering how much sleep the youngsters would get tonight. She hummed to herself as she got dressed, and brushed her hair until it bounced and shone like curly moonbeams. The warm summer air caressed her skin, and she slipped into a crisp sleeveless blouse and a lightweight wraparound skirt. With a sigh of anticipation, she dabbed on some cologne, then lowered herself into a lounge chair on the outside deck. In this rare quiet moment, she intended to think about the changes in her life and wait for Quentin's return.

It seemed like ages ago that she'd told him about the painful lessons she'd learned while married to Brent. She recalled her passionate outburst, telling Quentin how Brent had taken advantage of her, resulting in her need for independence.

And yet it was only a few days ago that they'd had that conversation. Had that woman disappeared? Not really, she mused. Not disappeared, just mellowed.

She leaned back in the lounge, a smile playing around her lips. It must be the onset of warm summer weather, she thought wryly, but she refused to think about Quentin leaving. He was here now, and she couldn't help but wonder where that might lead.

Headlights illuminated the marina for a moment as a car

drove into the parking lot. They were quickly extinguished, and she waited to hear the familiar crunch of gravel underfoot. She cocked her head but heard nothing. The silence was puzzling. A few moments later, the soft thud of a car door reached her ears and she stood up, alert now for the sound of the doorbell.

Movement caught her eye, and she realized that Quentin was making his way down the front lawn toward his houseboat, his steps stiff and wooden. She waited for the light to go on as he entered the boat, but it remained dark, bobbing peacefully in the black water beside the dock. Alarmed at this odd behavior, she flew down the steps and across the lawn.

The sliding door on the houseboat was still open, and she stepped onto the back deck, pausing at the entrance. "Quentin?" she called softly, then stepped into the cabin. Lights from the dock filtered through the side windows. He was sitting on the bench of the dining nook, head in his hands.

"Quentin?" she repeated. "Is everything all right?"

She slid into the booth across from him. This behavior was not like him at all. She tried to keep her voice light. "Did you have an argument with your father?"

He raised his head, anguish in his eyes and on his face. "My father has Alzheimer's," he said dully. "I don't even know if he recognized me."

Tears welled up in Julie's eyes but she made no effort to wipe them away. "Oh, Quentin," she whispered, and reached her hand across the table toward him.

He stared at her hand for a moment, then turned aside, long fingers massaging his head as though trying to scrub away the painful memories. "I should have been there for him," he said.

"I shouldn't have let him chase me away that last time." He tilted his head up, giving her a quick look, then dropped it again. "I don't know if I told you this, but I came up once to see him. It was about five years ago. He told me to go away, and like an idiot I let him run me off." His voice lowered to little more than a whisper. "I'll bet he knew what was happening and didn't want me to see him like that."

"But Quentin, how were you to know?" Julie's heart ached for him.

His head wagged back and forth. "I should have known."

He was being irrational, but his anguish was hard to watch. Julie stood up. "I'll make us a cup of tea." She moved toward the small kitchen.

His hand shot out and grabbed her by the wrist, pulling her closer. She leaned against him, wishing with all her heart that she could absorb some of his pain. His hand slid around her waist, holding her in a loose embrace, and she stroked his head, running her fingers through his sandy curls.

"I'm so sorry, Quentin." Her gaze was steady as she met his eyes. "If only things had turned out differently." He nodded and closed his eyes and she brushed her lips against his eyelids. "I don't know what to say."

He groaned and pulled her closer. "Don't say anything," he whispered, pulling her face down again to meet his.

Julie's senses reeled. His hands awakened longings that had been dormant for too long. She came alive as his lips met hers, every nerve ending in her body welcoming his touch. His strong arms held her safely and she relaxed, giving herself over to the pleasure of his kiss. This was not the young man who had given her a brief kiss one magical night many years ago. No . . . this was a mature, confident man who kissed her skillfully, threatening to buckle her knees.

He pulled back, and she wanted to grab him, to bring him back where he belonged, to taste more of his kisses. Instead, he stuck out a knee and pulled her down, until she sat on it, his arm holding her firmly.

"Should I say I'm sorry?" His eyes glinted in the dim light.

"No," she said, slipping an arm around his shoulders. His muscles twitched under her touch.

"Good." He cupped her chin with his free hand and kissed her lightly, his mouth moving under hers. "Do you know how long I've waited to do that?" His thumb brushed against her lips and then his fingers were in her hair. It was a good thing she was sitting down, because this time her legs would definitely have given out.

She looked into his eyes. "About as long as I've been waiting for you to come back."

A slow smile illuminated his face. "That's what I like about you, Julie." He paused. "Or should I say one of the things I like. You're so honest."

She gave him a sad smile. "Without honesty we don't have much, do we? I learned that the hard way."

He went very still for a moment, then nodded. "You're right," he said. "And I have something to tell you."

The tenderness of a few moments ago had been broken, and she longed to get it back. She placed two fingers against his lips. "Whatever it is, it can wait." She kissed him hungrily. "There'll be lots of time to talk later."

Quentin gathered her in his arms and kissed her until she was breathless. Then he pulled her against his chest, murmuring into her hair. Her heartbeat returned to normal, and reality came flooding back.

"Quentin," she said, pulling back reluctantly. "I'm so sorry about your father. Is there anything I can do?" She continued to stroke his head.

"Thanks, Julie, but this is something I have to figure out for myself." He gave her an odd look. "And that's not the only thing I need to figure out."

She was afraid to let herself hope. After all, Quentin Callahan was a sophisticated man, and they'd shared nothing more than a few kisses. But what kisses! She got unsteadily to her feet, reluctant to leave. "Then I'll leave you." She walked to the dock and turned to find him right behind her, a large, steady presence in her life.

"I'll say good night now." The moonlight was behind him, casting his face into shadows. It was disconcerting, not being able to see his eyes, and for a few seconds she wondered if she really knew him at all. The sudden thought was irrational; she knew that, but even so, goose bumps popped out on her skin.

"Good night, Julie." His voice was warm and husky, banishing her ridiculous notions. "I'll see you tomorrow."

Chapter Seven

Sunlight spilled through the window, waking Quentin with a start. For a moment he was disoriented, but the soft slap of water against the floats reminded him of where he was. He closed his eyes and fell back onto the pillow, trying to come to grips with yesterday's events.

He visualized his father shuffling down the hallway, and his stomach plunged. With an audible sigh he swung his legs out of bed, then sat there, scanning through memories of his past, the images stuttering like an old film. It was difficult to reconcile the large, belligerent man who'd been his father with the man in the care home. For a few years after his mother died the young Quentin had survived by recalling the good times they'd shared as a family. That had worked for a while, but those memories were soon erased by the actions of the angry, sullen man who never recovered from the grief of losing his wife. In a way, the misery of his teenage years was responsible for his current business success. Watching his father spiral downward into a world of drunken self-pity had strengthened his resolve to get as far away as possible—to be a self-made man. As the years passed, his anger had softened with the realization that his father had loved his mother and had been heartbroken over her death. But that knowledge had come too late to be of any comfort to the young, lost teenager.

He shoved himself up from the bed and stepped into the shower, turning his face to the cold blast that came out of the nozzle. There was nothing he could do to change the past. He hadn't pursued a relationship with his father, hadn't been there for him, but he would be there now, even if his father never recognized him again. He would visit Dr. Austen. It would be painful, but he owed it to himself to find out as much as possible about his father's condition and what he could do to help.

The warm water kicked in and he picked up the soap, bringing it to his nose. The scent was fresh and clean—like Julie. He leaned against the wall of the shower and let the water beat down on his back. It had taken all his strength to let her leave the boat last night. Even then, he'd almost run after her for one last embrace, one last kiss. He loved the way she looked up at him, her eyes trusting and full of love. He'd never known anyone like her before.

He stepped out of the shower and reached for the towel, his thoughts drifting back to his last relationship. Two years ago, he'd been engaged to a sleek, beautiful sales executive. When they'd walked into a room as a couple, heads turned. Belinda had possessed a sharp mind, and her love of sailing was equal to his. They had planned to buy a penthouse overlooking English Bay in Vancouver and were also considering a ski chalet in Whistler. They each had high-powered, stimulating careers, and for a while it seemed they were a perfect match. It took a leisurely holiday in a remote resort on the west coast of Vancouver Island to make him realize that they weren't compatible at all, that she was using him for his contacts. She'd given him a cool look when he ended their relationship, then moved on to her next conquest.

He shaved quickly, wondering what in the world had made him think of Belinda—it certainly wasn't because he missed her. Perhaps it was the contrast with Julie, with her sweet nature. He grinned into the mirror. Yes, Julie was sweet, but she had developed an inner strength that was as remarkable as it was appealing. And she was causing him to reexamine what was important in his life.

Footsteps sounded on the dock and he glanced outside. Today's schedule was full, and Carl was already at work. Quentin wasn't sure when he could find time to be alone with Julie, but he needed to see her and tell her the truth about why he was here.

Julie fumbled groggily for her alarm, then forced herself to get up and look out the window, a habit of many years. Sunlight danced on the water, reflecting splinters of light into her eyes. Shielding her face, she stepped back behind the curtain just as Quentin came out onto the back deck of *Chickadee*, a mug of coffee in his hand. He waved at Carl with his free hand, then turned and looked up toward the house. Her heart lurched at the sight of him—tall, confident, and 100 percent male. Was it any wonder she'd fantasized about him for years after he'd left to pursue his studies? She wasn't a teenager anymore, but the woman she had become was more attracted to him than ever.

He walked down the dock and exchanged a few words with Carl. He'd only been here a few days, and he was already a valuable member of the team. Not to mention the fact that in his arms she'd come alive for the first time in years.

"Don't go there," she told herself aloud. "He has his own problems to take care of, and besides, he's only here for a few weeks." Her mind whirled as she tried to sort out her emotions while planning for the busy day ahead. They had five new charters leaving today and four boats returning. She showered quickly, then pulled on a T-shirt screened with the company logo and walked into the living room. The marina lay spread out below, and Carl and Quentin were already at work fueling the departing units. She watched for a few moments, then with a shake of her head she went downstairs into the office, where the telephones were already ringing.

"Good morning, Maggie," she called, and crossed the room to pick up one of the lines. The caller wanted to rent a large boat, and she regretfully informed him that their only large units were booked for the dates he wanted. Another indication that she needed to expand her fleet, and it was only the first call of the morning. She took a deep breath, sensing that it was going to be a long day.

"You look different today, Jules." Maggie crossed to the coffeemaker. "What have you been up to?"

"About 5'4"." Julie gave the standard answer.

"Oh, ha, ha!" Maggie's brow furrowed.

Julie tried not to crumble under the close scrutiny of her friend. "Not much," she said, trying to sound casual.

Maggie whirled around and crossed the room. "Oh no you don't," she said, leaning over Julie's desk. "You're blushing, and that can mean only one thing. You've had a close encounter with our new maintenance man." She waggled her eyebrows. "So tell me, how was he?"

"Maggie!" Julie glanced around as though someone might be listening. "What a thing to say."

"Uh-oh. You're waffling, my friend, and I don't know if that's a good sign or a bad one. I mean, since your divorce there hasn't been anyone else, so I don't know how to read you."

Julie poured herself a cup of coffee, stalling for time while she collected her thoughts. She and Maggie had been friends since they were children. It was unlikely that she would be able to hide her feelings much longer, and to tell the truth, she wanted to confide in her best friend. She began to pace back and forth in front of her friend's desk.

"I think I'm falling in love with him, Mags. Can you believe it? Me, falling in love, after all those lectures I gave myself when he came back?"

"What lectures?"

"Oh, you know. How I'm independent. How I'm never going to let a man take advantage of me again." She shot her friend a despairing look. "I shouldn't let this happen when I know perfectly well he's going back home."

She sank down on a chair facing Maggie's desk and exhaled slowly. "It's like a dream come true, Mags. He's everything I thought, and more." Her voice trailed away.

The normally glib Maggie was at a loss for words. "So what happens now?"

"I don't know. It's like some sort of fantasy. Things like this don't happen to me. This man was my knight in shining armor when I was a kid, and I dreamed about him for years." She smiled sheepishly. "Even when I was married, I would think about him when things got bad." She looked around the office, focusing on familiar items. "And now he shows up in my real world, and I find him even more exciting than I remembered. He takes my breath away, Maggie."

"Well, that's good," said Maggie, recovering somewhat. "After all, we don't want you falling for some jerk, do we? I mean, on a scale of one to ten, this guy's definitely a twelve. He's the complete package."

"Oh, yeah." Julie smiled to herself. "He sure is." She slapped her head. "My gosh, I almost forgot to tell you. He went to visit his father yesterday, and he has Alzheimer's."

"He didn't know?"

"No, it was a real shock." Julie could still see the bleak expression in Quentin's eyes when he'd told her. "I don't think it's completely sunk in yet. When I left him last night, he said he had a lot of thinking to do. It's a bit late now for both of them, but I think he intends to help out however he can."

Maggie nodded. "I wouldn't expect any less, even though his father was mean as a snake when Quentin was young." Julie gave her a startled look, but Maggie continued. "Everyone knew."

The door flew open and Nick came bounding in, his sleeping bag over his shoulder. "Hi, Maggie. Hi, Mom." He stood on the balls of his feet, eyes bright with excitement.

Julie's heart softened at the sight of her son. "Hi, yourself. Did you have fun last night?"

"Yeah, it was neat." He placed his sleeping bag on the chair beside Julie's desk. "We cooked over the fire and we ate a whole bag of marshmallows. I need a new battery for my flashlight, Mom." He ran to the window and looked out over the marina. "Do you think Quentin could give me that lesson today?"

Julie gave him a blank look. "What lesson?"

"He said he'd help me with my swimming. I'm going to go for my senior swimmers badge at camp, and Quentin said he could give me some tips."

Julie shook her head. "I don't know about that, Nick. I guess you'll have to ask him. This is the first I've heard of it."

"Us guys don't have to tell you everything, Mom." Nick shoved his hands in his back pockets and Julie had to look away to hide her smile. She'd seen them talking together yesterday, and now Nick was emulating Quentin's pose. "We talked about it when we were working."

Julie turned back to him, barely managing to keep a straight face. "Well then, I guess you'll have to ask him, won't you?"

"Okay." He started down the stairs.

"Take your sleeping bag upstairs, Nicky. This is an office, remember?"

With a dramatic rolling of his eyes, Nick did as he was told, and the sound of pounding feet could be heard a few moments later as he ran down the outside stairs to the lawn and onto the dock.

"Looks like lover boy has made more than one conquest," observed Maggie as Nick accosted Quentin on the dock.

Julie refused to take the bait. "He seems pretty good with him, I must say." She returned to her desk. "If I recall correctly, your friends are coming back from their charter today. Have you heard anything?"

Maggie raised an eyebrow. "He called this morning from the boat. We're going for drinks and dinner right after work."

The telephone started ringing again, and Maggie turned to answer, waving a bank deposit book in Julie's direction.

Nodding, Julie took it and picked up her keys. This morning would be a perfect opportunity to do the banking and go to the grocery store to stock up on food before her family started to arrive. With so many customers arriving this afternoon, this might be her only chance to get organized before the onslaught.

She stepped out into the sunshine and automatically looked down toward the dock, where Nick was "helping" Quentin. Her son's enthusiastic chatter carried clearly, but she could not make out Quentin's quiet replies. Smiling with contentment, she turned toward the parking lot.

"Excuse me, Mrs. Chapman. Could I talk to you for a minute, please?"

Startled, Julie turned to see Jason Armstrong standing on the path leading from the parking lot to the office.

"Why, hello, Jason. How are you?" The young man had been lured away by Apex Houseboats several weeks previously, and he appeared nervous, his gaze darting around self-consciously.

"I'm all right, I guess." He looked toward the dock, which was crowded with cleaning carts and maintenance equipment. "I wanted to let you know that I'm not working for Apex anymore, and I was wondering if you would consider hiring me back when you need help."

Julie frowned. "What happened, Jason?"

"Well, ma'am. They promised us big wages and everything, but they have so many people over there, we aren't getting very many hours." His prepared speech tumbled out, and he finally looked directly at Julie. "They aren't very nice people, Mrs. Chapman. I never should have left here."

Julie nodded. "And are you sure you're not going to leave us in the lurch again when things get busier next door?" She was thrilled at the idea of more help, but she couldn't afford any more disappointments.

"Oh, no, ma'am. I've learned my lesson." He paused. "Wayne Jenkins is in the car with me. He'd like to come back too."

Julie smiled and the young man visibly relaxed. "It's fine with me, Jason, but the both of you will have to go down and talk to Carl. You can tell him what I said, but he has to approve. He's in charge of maintenance, so it's his call."

The young man's face was wreathed in smiles as he headed back toward the parking lot. "I won't let you down, ma'am," he called over his shoulder. "You'll see."

"I believe you," she said to herself as she climbed into her car. "And I also believe things are starting to look up."

Julie returned from her errands in time to assist Maggie with the afternoon arrivals. The dock was crowded with excited renters unloading their supplies. Carl had wasted no time putting Jason and Wayne to work, and the young men were assisting the customers as they boarded their reserved boats.

Julie murmured to Carl as they passed on the dock, "I see you have some extra help today."

"I decided to start them right away, to let them know there are no hard feelings." Carl's fairness in dealing with the staff was well known. He'd been dismayed when the youngsters had left to work next door, but he was too experienced to let his personal feelings stand in the way of re-hiring qualified maintenance men. "They tell me that Steve will probably be quitting soon as well. We could use him, Julie."

She laid a hand on his arm. "Do whatever you think is

best. You know I trust you." As she spoke she looked around, trying not to be too obvious. "I don't see Quentin."

"He took Nick for some swimming lessons. The kid was pestering him all morning, but Callahan made him work for a couple of hours to make up the time." Carl laughed. "At least that's what Quentin told him. He sure knows how to build up the kid's confidence."

"I hate to admit it, but I hadn't given much thought to how much he needs a man in his life. It's clear to see how much he likes hanging around with Quentin."

Carl turned thoughtful. "Odd, isn't it? Quentin's only been back a few days, but it's like he's always been here. It would be great if he could stick around, 'cause I enjoy working with him, but I know that's only wishful thinking. I'll miss him when he leaves."

You and me both, thought Julie, then looked away when tears pooled in her eyes, threatening to spill over. "I'll miss him too," she said, rubbing her arms. "It's been like old times." She wandered off, looking for some tough, physical work to occupy her hands, if not her mind. The cleaning crew was finishing up on a returned boat and she pitched in, offering to clean out the hot tub on the top deck.

She climbed the ladder and started working, determined to find a quiet hour this evening to sort out her feelings. In spite of what had passed between them last night, there had been no promises, no plans for the future. The truth was that she could not change the facts. Quentin's life was in Vancouver. He was a business consultant, not a part-time helper at a houseboat company, and it was time she faced up to the inevitable.

She finished the cleanup and was performing one last check of the boat as the renters trundled down the dock with their supplies. They were the last arrivals of the day, and a peaceful calm settled over the dock as they pulled out and headed slowly out into Shuswap Lake, respecting the NO WAKE signs posted along the Narrows.

"That was a good day." Carl appeared beside her, a container of hydraulic fluid in his hand and a satisfied grin on his face. "It's great to have so many rentals at this time of year."

"If business keeps up like this, we'll be able to order those new units for next year." Julie glanced at Carl, watching for his reaction. "Even if we have to get rid of some of the older boats, I think we need to do it to keep up with the big boys." She jerked her head toward their neighbor to the west.

"I suppose larger boats would be nice. You and Maggie have more of an idea of what the customers are asking for, but what I'd like is more space." He looked at the docks on either side of them. "There are lots of ways we could utilize more space, but there's no way we can rearrange things here."

Carl rarely volunteered his opinion, and Julie wanted to encourage him. "What would you do with extra space?" she asked. "Besides room for more boats, that is?"

The older man took off his cap and ran a hand over his balding head. "Well," he said, "I've often thought how convenient it would be if we had a stripped-down boat where we could store all of our supplies. When we get the maintenance carts and the housekeeping carts on the dock at the same time, we barely have room for the customers, not to mention their supplies."

"What a great idea," said Julie. "I'd never have thought of that. Personally, I'd buy a small pre-fab building and start a little store. People always want last-minute things before they leave. We could also rent games and DVDs, now that we don't provide them for free anymore." She glanced over at Apex Houseboats again. "Maybe I should make an offer to buy *them*," she said with a wry grin.

"Yeah, right." Carl's expression made it clear what he thought about their neighbors. "By the way, have you heard any more from those clowns about trying to buy you out?"

"No, thank goodness." She took a few steps toward the end of the dock and looked up and down the Narrows. "Who'd have thought that this strip of land would become so valuable? It's narrow, there's a limited view, and there's constant boat traffic."

Carl nodded his head in the other direction. "And it's close to the Trans Canada Highway. I wish I'd had the foresight to buy some property twenty years ago."

"Then I'd be on my hands and knees, begging to buy it." Julie laughed, then quickly sobered. "I'd probably end up in a bidding war with our neighbors."

Carl glanced at her in mock horror. "No way. I wouldn't deal with them on a bet."

Julie smiled. "Thanks, Carl." She turned thoughtful. "The way they treated those boys was shameful."

"I'm glad to have them back. Oh, I almost forgot. Jason and Wayne are working tomorrow as well, since Quentin wants to visit old Doc Austen. Terrible about his father, isn't it?"

"Yes. I don't know how I'd react if anything like that happened in our family. We should give thanks more often for our good health."

"You've got that right. Well, good night, Julie. See you in the morning."

"Good night, Carl." Julie wandered onto the lawn and eased herself up onto the stone wall that surrounded the weeping willow. Two rocks stuck out from the wall and she settled her feet on them, thinking of the times that she'd sat in this exact spot when she was young, watching the ospreys fishing in the clear waters. This was her favorite time of day, when the sun slanted through the willow, painting golden streaks across the lawn. The chatter of an oriole sounded nearby, and she made a mental note to set out some lengths of string to aid them with their nest building. The nest pouches, tucked in among the willow branches in the summer months, would become visible in the winter—mute reminders of their too brief summer visit.

Julie kicked her sneakers against the wall, just as she'd done in her youth. Back then, summer had never been long enough. Now it started in May with a flurry of activity as early customers began to arrive—a preview of the busy months to come.

She thought back to the days when her parents operated the business with only six boats. She'd loved the business from the beginning, and as she grew older she found herself in charge of cleaning the boats and preparing them for new customers. She especially enjoyed the small personal touches that brought guests back year after year. She bought sturdy stoneware vases that wouldn't tip over and filled them with wildflowers. She stocked special animal treats for those returning guests with cats or dogs. When rain was forecast, she placed suitable videos on board for families with children. These small gestures were appreciated by the guests, and within a few years, SunBird became known as the company with personal service and friendly staff.

At that time, the joy of renting a houseboat on Shuswap

Lake was relatively unknown, and a renter could motor off into one of the arms of the lake, find an unoccupied beach, and stay undisturbed for several days. Today it was considerably busier, but still a desirable way to spend a vacation, as evidenced by the increasing numbers of boats every year.

Mike had never been enthusiastic about hanging around the dock. Along with Quentin, who was hired as soon as the season started, they'd done their chores cheerfully, but their real interest lay in exploring the lake in Mike's canoe. One summer they pooled their money and bought a small sailboat. She smiled as she recalled the two gangly youths, all arms and legs and energy—proud owners setting off in their small boat.

Looking back, those days had been idyllic, almost like living in a dream world. Julie sighed. It was time to get back to reality, even if she ended up with a broken heart. After all, everyone knows that dreams don't come true.

Chapter Eight

That's it, Nick. You're doing fine." Quentin stood in the water and watched while Nick practiced the breaststroke. "Keep kicking your legs and pull, pull." Their towels and clothes lay in a pile on the beach; they had been working steadily for an hour.

"That's enough for today." He smiled as the youngster's feet found the bottom and he adjusted his trunks. "You're doing really well. Just remember not to rush your strokes, and you'll do fine."

Nick's voice was muffled as he dried his hair. "Do you think I'll pass the test, Quentin?" He looped the towel around his neck and looked up with eager eyes. "Do you think I'm good enough?"

"It's not up to me to say, sport, but I think you'll do just fine. You're a natural in the water."

Nick sat down and burrowed into the warm sand, obviously not wanting the afternoon to end. Quentin sat beside him and pulled on his T-shirt, grateful for the warmth of the sun.

"What was my Mom like when she was a kid? You knew her back then, didn't you?"

The question startled Quentin, and he glanced sideways at Nick, who was gazing straight out at the lake. "Yes, I knew her. When I first met her she was younger than us, and we used to call her Squirt 'cause she was so small." He paused. "Why do you ask?"

"I don't know." Nick poked at the sand. "She usually doesn't laugh very much, but she seems a lot happier since you got here." His brown eyes were solemn. "But you're leaving again, aren't you?"

Quentin had a hard time swallowing. A knot had formed in his throat.

"Where did you hear that?" He was scrambling for time, trying to decide what to say.

"I heard Carl telling Jason and Wayne." He edged away, so he could look up at his hero. "Is it true?"

"Yes, Nick. That was my plan when I got here, but . . ."

Nick leaped up and gathered his clothes. "I have to get dressed now," he said, his voice tight. "Thanks for the lesson." He ran to the change room, his towel trailing on the ground.

Quentin lowered his head and massaged the back of his neck. The look on Nick's face was troubling, but how could he tell the child what he was going to do until he knew for sure himself? A cloud covered the sun as he pulled on his tracksuit and wandered over to the parking lot to wait for Nick. The swimming lesson had been an enjoyable interlude, but the time had arrived for some serious thinking.

They drove home in silence, with Nick darting cautious looks at Quentin. They pulled into the parking lot and Quentin placed a hand on Nick's shoulder, trying to recapture the closeness they'd shared earlier. "Shall we try for another lesson before you go to camp?"

"Yeah, sure, that would be cool." The youngster opened the door and clambered out quickly, disappearing in the direction of the house. Quentin sighed and got out more slowly. His life was becoming very complicated.

Rounding the corner onto the lawn, he caught sight of Julie sitting hunched on the rock wall and his heart swelled. He paused to enjoy the sight of her, her slender figure appearing childlike. She sat in a pose he recalled from their youth, feet resting on the protruding rocks. She used to call them "footstones," and he smiled, his earlier chill replaced by the warmth of the memory.

"Hiya, Squirt," he said softly. "I didn't see you around very much today." She turned her head and his heart thundered in his chest when he looked at her.

"Quentin," she said, her voice barely more than a whisper. The magnetic pull of her gaze drew him the last few steps across the lawn until he stood in front of her. Reaching out, he traced the outline of her jaw with his fingers, then dropped his hand. The next time he kissed her he wanted it to mean something. But first, he needed to decide what was happening in his life.

A shadow of disappointment flickered across her eyes, but she recovered quickly. "Where's Nick?" she asked. "Carl said you were going to give him a swimming lesson."

"I did. He ran into the house." He raised his head as the youngster came thundering down the stairs. "Here he is now, in case you hadn't heard."

"Hi, Mom. When are we going to have dinner?" Nick seemed to have recovered from his earlier funk. "Quentin says I just need to keep practicing."

Julie's eyes were full of love for her son. "I knew you'd be great," she said proudly.

Nick tugged at her hand. "Come on, Mom. I'm starving."

"All right, let's go and see what we can find to eat. I went shopping today, so it shouldn't be too hard." The pair went up the steps to the house while Nick regaled her with stories of his prowess in the water.

At the stop of the stairs she turned back toward Quentin, mouthed a silent "Thank you," then turned and disappeared into the house.

The cabin of the houseboat was hot and stuffy. Quentin opened all the windows, grabbed a bottle of water, and stepped out onto the rear deck. Without conscious thought, he checked the remaining unrented boats to ensure that they were all secure. Funny how he'd come to care about the business so quickly. His experience in the corporate world was far removed from this, but since his arrival he was constantly amazed at how content he was. There was a surprising amount of satisfaction to be gained from the everyday chores of maintaining the equipment and assisting the customers. The houseboat rental business dealt with people on a more personal level. For many customers, renting a houseboat was the holiday of a lifetime, and he was proud to be a part of the company that made their dreams come true. Even if it was only for a few weeks longer.

With a comfortable sense of belonging, he picked up his deck chair and made his way to the end of the dock. The early evening sun bounced off the rippled surface of the Narrows, bathing his face in reflected light. He pulled his cap lower to shade his eyes, thinking of the enormous changes in his life in such a short time.

It had been a mistake not to tell Julie his reason for coming here. He should have told her right away—that first night—but he'd been afraid that she would pull back from him, regard him as the enemy. And now look where he was! As recently as last night she'd told him how she felt about honesty. He took a slug of water. What had she said? *Without honesty we don't have much.* She was right, and his failure to disclose his reason for being here was tantamount to lying.

His eyes narrowed as he drank again and considered his own life. Speaking of the truth, if he were honest with himself, he would admit that he no longer enjoyed the type of work he'd been doing for the past six years. He'd been so focused on success that he hadn't realized it was eating away at his soul. All he did was help large corporations make more money. In the business world, nobody shook your hand and told you how much they enjoyed watching the ospreys dive for fish; nobody told you of the simple pleasure of sitting around the campfire with family, telling ghost stories and roasting marshmallows.

And speaking of honesty, he'd also acknowledge that when he looked at Julie, his heart expanded with an almost indescribable joy, that he could be happy for the rest of his life if she and Nick were by his side.

And with the greatest regret, he would admit that he should have made more of an effort to make peace with his father. That was something he couldn't change now, but he could still be a good son, even if his father never recognized him again.

Sitting there in the golden light, his mind was at peace for the first time in years. He knew what he had to do. Now that the staffing problems were sorted out, he would be free to leave in a few days. He would go back to Vancouver, to his business, and sort things out. Then he would come back here and tell Julie everything. He stared into the water, not caring if anyone saw the satisfied grin on his face. Life was suddenly so much brighter.

Julie walked into the living room, drying her hands on the tea towel. Quentin was sitting there again, and she knew she might not get a better chance to clear up any misunderstandings about last night. She tossed down the tea towel and ran downstairs.

"May I join you?"

Quentin jumped up, knocking over the deck chair in his haste. "I was just thinking about you."

"Is that good or bad?" She tried to gauge his mood but couldn't see his eyes under the brim of his cap.

He pushed the cap back and a tentative smile played around his lips. "Here, let me get you a chair." He grabbed one from the back deck of the nearest boat.

"You go first," she said, moving her chair squarely in front of him before sitting down.

Quentin removed his cap and raked his fingers through his hair. His eyes were serious and a tiny shiver of worry crept down her spine, but she maintained her composure. The water, the passing boats, the sounds of people laughing all faded into the background as she waited for him to speak.

"Julie, I owe you an apology for last night. I—I never should have grabbed you like that." His eyes pleaded with her. "I don't know what came over me. Forgive me, please?"

Hadn't he known how much she'd enjoyed being in his arms? "Forgive you?" she said, her voice cracking. "There's nothing to forgive." She pulled at a loose thread on her shorts. "Was it really so bad, Quentin?"

"Are you kidding?" A fleeting smile lit up his eyes. "I enjoyed every minute of it, but the timing was all wrong. I think we both know that."

"You're right. You were definitely in shock." She leaned forward. "But I don't normally act like that, and I wanted you to know." She gave a short, mirthless laugh. "What am I saying? I haven't even dated since the divorce. . . ." She stopped short. "Why am I telling you all this? You don't need to hear about my love life, or lack of it." She hung her head. "Oh, boy. This is not going well at all."

Quentin took her hands in his. "Listen to me, Julie. You were there for me last night, and I appreciate it." He looked directly into her eyes. "But things are a little complicated right now."

She inhaled sharply, realizing that she'd been holding her breath. "I understand. This thing with your dad—it caught us both by surprise. But last night? I'm not sorry it happened."

"Neither am I, but right now I need a few days to sort some things out." A sailboat slid by and he watched it for a few moments before turning back to her. "Did Carl tell you I'm taking time off tomorrow? I'm going to visit Dr. Austen, then possibly visit my dad again." He looked away and when he spoke it was almost as though he were talking to himself. "I need to hear what the doc has to say." He picked up the empty water bottle and his fingers tightened around it, collapsing the plastic. "It's difficult knowing that his condition can't be reversed. It makes me feel so helpless."

Her heart ached for him. "But you came back. Think how

badly you'd feel if you'd never learned about his condition." She reached out, touched him briefly on the knee. "There'll be something you can do, Quentin. I know it."

He relaxed his grip on the water bottle and stood, pulling her up with him. "You're a glass half full kinda girl, aren't you?" He walked slowly up the dock.

"I guess so." She matched her steps to his.

"That's my girl." They continued walking in silence until they stood outside his houseboat.

Julie forced herself not to look up, lest he see the longing in her eyes. "Good night, Quentin," she said softly. "Have a good day tomorrow."

"You too," he said, then stepped onto the back deck of his temporary home.

She knew he was watching her as she made her way slowly up the lawn. Even though she could almost feel his gaze boring into her back, she didn't turn around. It wouldn't do to let him see the tears of disappointment rolling down her face. Squaring her shoulders, she ran the last few steps up to the house. Things would look brighter tomorrow.

"Did you turn on the valve, sir?" Maggie was dealing with a recurring "problem" when Julie walked into the office the next morning. "Yes, sir, the valve that turns on the propane. I'll wait while you try that." She busied herself at her computer while she waited for the customer to try the barbecue. Julie noticed that her friend was wearing her usual flamboyant attire. It was a relief to see that at least one thing in her life was back to normal.

"That's all right, sir. It happens all the time." Maggie hung up and turned to Julie. "Another one who thought the barbecue was broken." She threw up her hands. "Don't they have barbecues at home? Can't they read the instructions? Or do their brains leak out when they go on holiday?"

"And good morning to you too." Julie poured herself a coffee, then went to stand by the window. It was good to see that Carl had a full complement of helpers, all in their SunBird T-shirts and busy with the boats. She waited for a comeback from Maggie, but was greeted by silence.

She walked back to her desk and glanced across the room. "What's the matter, Mags? Cat got your tongue?" That would surely get her friend going.

"Yeah, I guess so."

Something was wrong here. Julie tried to jog her memory for what might be bothering her friend, then slapped the heel of her hand against her forehead. "Oh, Mags, I'm sorry. I forgot to ask you about your date with the lawyer last night. How did it go?"

"It was okay. We had a nice dinner, but it didn't take me long to realize that we don't have much in common." She looked into her coffee mug and seemed surprised to find it empty. "Funny thing is, I don't think he even realized it. He was too busy talking about himself the whole time. I scarcely got a word in edgewise." She examined her brightly painted nails. "Even worse than that, the guy never reads for pleasure! Can you believe it?" Maggie, a voracious reader, had little patience for those who didn't read. "I suppose he's a decent enough guy, but he's just not for me. At least I found that out sooner rather than later."

Maggie's tone was harsh, bitter almost, and Julie gave her a sharp look. There was something else—something her friend wasn't telling her. "That's not the whole story, Mags. What's the matter?"

Maggie turned to Julie, her expression bleak. "It's not good."

"For heaven's sake, it can't be that terrible. Out with it."

"All right." Maggie braced herself, elbows on her desk. "Remember how I told you before that Palmer said he'd seen Quentin around, but couldn't remember where?" Julie nodded. "Well, he remembered, and you aren't going to like it."

A chill of apprehension ran down Julie's spine. "What else can go wrong?" she said, almost to herself.

"What's that supposed to mean?" Maggie's concern was immediate.

Julie started pacing. "I talked to Quentin last night and he apologized." She paused and gave her head a quick shake. "He actually apologized for the previous night, as if he'd done something wrong."

"What did you say?"

"Basically I told him that there was nothing to apologize for, and that I didn't regret it." She stopped and looked out the window, her gaze coming to rest on *Chickadee*. "You know, it's almost funny. I realized later that what I really wanted was for him to sweep me up in his arms and tell me that we'd live happily ever after. Some fantasy, huh?" She didn't wait for a response. "Instead, he told me that he needs time to sort some things out. I mean, I understand that the news about his father came as a shock, but he knows there isn't a lot he can do about that. He said all the right things, but it was still a brush-off."

"I'm sorry, Julie, but what I have to tell you won't make you feel any better."

Julie groaned. "It couldn't be any worse."

Maggie didn't answer, and Julie waited for her to continue, dreading what might be coming but needing to know.

Maggie tapped some papers with a pen. "Palmer does some specialized work for Delahunt Holdings."

"The people who own Apex? No wonder you didn't like him."

Maggie examined the pen, unable to meet her friend's eyes. "Julie, what he remembered is that he'd seen Quentin at Delahunt. Several times, in fact. Evidently, Quentin's the one they send out when they want to take over another company. Palmer says they call him their 'ace in the hole,' because he rarely lets them down."

Julie gave Maggie a blank look. "Quentin works for Delahunt? No, Maggie. Your friend must be mistaken." She glanced down at the dock, even though she knew he wasn't there. "Quentin would have said something."

"You'd think so, wouldn't you?" Maggie's gaze was steady. "There's no mistake, Jules. He even remembered his name, and the fact that his briefcase had his initials embossed in gold. 'Q.C.,' he said. I grilled him about it for as long as I could without arousing suspicion. It's Quentin, all right."

Julie clutched at the window frame. Random thoughts bounced around inside her head, scraps of remembered conversations intermingled with memories of Quentin, smiling confidently as he offered to help her out. This couldn't be happening. And yet . . .

She turned to Maggie. "You're sure?"

Her friend nodded, unable to speak.

The door opened and Carl stepped inside. He looked from Maggie to Julie. "Could I speak to you for a minute, Julie?" he asked.

He seemed uncomfortable, but Julie didn't notice. She pulled herself together and smiled in what she hoped was a convincing manner. "Sure, Carl. What is it?"

"Well . . ." He gestured out the window toward the bustling dock. "Steve came back to work this morning, and he just told me something strange." He glanced over at Maggie, then continued. "He started telling me about what they said over at Apex when he quit."

"I don't know if I want to hear this right now," said Julie distractedly. "Is it important?"

Carl's face reflected his indecision. "I don't know. But when he told them he was leaving, they said it didn't matter because they had someone on the inside over here at Sun-Bird."

Julie bit her lower lip to keep from speaking. She trusted Carl implicitly, but she couldn't bring herself to discuss the situation with him right now. Her world was crashing down around her, and she couldn't deal with one more thing.

"Thanks, Carl," she said, managing to meet his eyes. By some miracle, her voice sounded normal when she spoke. "After what those people have done this summer, I don't know if I believe anything they say, but thanks for letting me know. After all, who could it be?"

The mechanic thought for a moment, then relief flooded his face. "Of course. You're right." He took off his cap and scratched the top of his head. "That's a relief, especially now that we're getting back on track with the maintenance."

"Don't worry about them," she said, sounding much more confident that she felt. "They're just disappointed that their little schemes haven't worked."

"Yeah," said Carl, obviously relieved. "Well, I'll get back down to the dock."

Maggie looked at her friend. "That was some performance, but why didn't you say anything? You always take Carl into your confidence."

Julie stood gazing out over the marina. Everything looked far away, as though she were looking through the wrong end of a pair of binoculars. She wondered idly if Maggie could hear her heart breaking. Or was that noise a door slamming shut inside her, protecting her from the turbulent emotions that threatened to erupt and sweep away the last vestiges of her self-control?

"Know what?" She turned to Maggie. "I need to get away for a while and clear my head. I'm going to take *Streak* and go for a ride. Can you hold down the fort for a while?"

"Of course." Maggie made shooing motions. "Take your time."

The marina kept a powerful runabout for emergencies, laughingly called *Blue Streak* by the employees. Getting away for a few hours might not solve her problems, but right now it was just what she needed.

Maggie rose and gave her friend a quick hug, fighting back her own tears. "I'll be here to listen when you get back," she said simply.

Julie walked briskly down the dock, smiling and nodding as staff and a few customers greeted her along the way. Carl noticed her heading for the runabout, and came over to cast off the lines. He gave her a thumbs-up and she eased the boat away from the dock. Staff from other houseboat companies called out to her as she motored out of the Narrows, chafing at the speed restrictions. She understood the need for them, as a large wake could damage the closely moored boats, but she was impatient to get away from everything that reminded her of Quentin. She scarcely noticed the intense blue of the sky, or the perfect white clouds that hung over the distant hills.

Once under the bridges and out into the lake, she pushed the throttle forward, standing up as the boat responded with a surge of power. The wind whipped through her hair and brought tears to her eyes as the boat cut eagerly through the water. She brushed them away and continued past the floating store, where several houseboats were tied up, buying supplies and gas.

The pounding in her head slowly eased and she throttled back, surprised at how fast she'd been going. Keenly aware of the importance of safe boating, she scolded herself for speeding. The sleek runabout leveled off, and she sat down behind the wheel, scouting the familiar shoreline. Construction on several new homes had started since her last trip up the lake and she frowned, trying to remember when that had been. Had running the business really taken over her life to such an extent that she hadn't indulged in one of her favorite pastimes? Boating had always been a pleasure, both with her parents and then again in the early days with Brent. These days, many more houseboats dotted the shores at night, but there were always plenty of sites where locals could stop, build a fire, and have a picnic. She wondered if Nick missed the picnics they used to have as a family, and vowed to ask him tonight.

A loon was fishing close by, where a stream fed into the lake. She watched as the bird slipped gracefully under the surface. She could see it swimming underwater, its speckled back clearly visible amid the tiny bubbles rising from between its feathers. The sight of the bird seemed to signify that everything was right in the world, and she found herself relaxing. Turning the boat, she shut off the motor and glided into shore, then kicked off her sneakers and jumped out onto a small beach where it was unlikely that she would be disturbed.

She tied the mooring rope to the roots of a beached log, then sat down and leaned back against the trunk. Dappled sunlight filtered through the birches on shore, warming her skin while she permitted herself to think about Maggie's and Carl's revelations.

She was calmer now, but that didn't make the knowledge any less painful. Staring out at the water, she was overcome by a profound sense of loss. Loss of faith in her own judgment—as a business owner and as a woman. In a few short days, Quentin had turned her life upside down. He'd changed the way she viewed the world, making her believe that she could give her heart again and bask in the glow of love freely returned. Tears ran down her face and she let them flow until they finally stopped. Dabbing her eyes with the hem of her blouse, she looked around. Nothing had changed. The world was still turning, the sun was still shining. With a wan smile she picked up a handful of pebbles, then watched as they slipped through her fingers, her mind far away.

Had she missed the signs? She couldn't believe that she had misjudged Quentin so badly. From the moment he'd come back into her life, he'd been supportive and caring. But Maggie was certain of her facts. Julie knew her friend well enough to know that she wouldn't have said anything unless she was absolutely sure.

She scoured her memory for the few times she and Quentin had talked about Apex. She seemed to recall that he had asked her if they'd made an offer in writing, but other than that, his comments had been minimal. As a matter of fact, he'd seemed pleased when she told him she wasn't interested. If he'd come back to influence her, wouldn't he have pointed out the pros and cons of selling to them—with emphasis on the pros?

Was she letting her heart rule her head? Closing her eyes, she remembered the night he'd learned about his father's condition. She'd never forget the safety of his arms, or the sweetness of his kisses. Just thinking about it now sent a warm glow through her body.

With a brisk shake of her head she forced herself to focus on the problem at hand. Quentin's specialty was in assessing takeover targets, and Delahunt/Apex wanted to buy her business. That much was a fact. But he had expressed his misgivings about continuing to work for his biggest client. He hadn't named them, but it was undoubtedly Delahunt. She stared out over the water, paying little attention to the houseboats moving toward their overnight positions along the shoreline. Something didn't add up, she thought to herself, but she couldn't put her finger on it.

She leaned against the log and drank in the sweet summer air as it skipped off the water. Tilting her head back, she looked up into the trees, watching the gilded leaves fluttering overhead. Their movement was almost hypnotic, and she closed her eyes, permitting her thoughts to drift as the gentle sounds of water slapped against her boat.

With a rush that was almost physical, memories flooded over her with astonishing clarity. Mike and Quentin as teenagers, splashing each other with hoses as they washed down the boats. Quentin's angry face as he rescued her on graduation night, and the desire that lurked behind his eyes as his lips met hers—the first real kiss she'd ever experienced.

Nick and Quentin working together on the dock, Nick's young chest swelling with pride at an obvious compliment. And Quentin's eyes, holding hers as he pulled her head down for a kiss.

Why these thoughts, and why now? The answer was simple. More than anything in her life, she wanted to believe in Quentin, in his integrity. In that moment, she made a decision. Rather than confront him with what she knew, she wanted him to prove to her, by his own actions, that her trust in him was not misplaced.

She scrambled up and untied the mooring rope, her mind made up. She pushed off, eager to return to the office and see what Maggie thought of her idea.

Chapter Nine

I don't know." Maggie's concern was evident. "Are you making this decision with your head or with your heart?"

Julie pointed at her friend. "I knew you'd ask me that, Mags, and the answer is yes."

"Very funny. Thanks a lot."

"Okay, okay. But I'm trying to see things from all sides." Maggie leaned forward to speak and Julie held up her hands. "It's not that I don't believe what your friend told you, because he has no reason to deceive you. But I also want to hang on to the hope that there's something else going on here. When you get right down to it, what have we got to lose?"

"No, Julie." Maggie shook her head. "What have *you* got to lose. That's what's important. This is your livelihood, and I can't believe you're not acting like the sharp businesswoman I know you to be."

Julie searched for the words to make her friend understand. "Listen to me, Mags—please. You of all people know we're doing well. That's true, isn't it?"

Maggie nodded. "Yes, but—"

"Stay with me here." Julie gave her friend a reassuring smile. "They can't buy my company if I don't want to sell, right?"

"Yes, but they can *make* you want to sell it. That's what concerns me."

"They've already tried that, and it didn't work." She cast about for some words to convince her friend. "Has anything bad happened since Quentin got here? Come on, be honest—has anything at all happened?"

Maggie shook her head. "No."

"All right. Now hear me out." Julie wandered around the office, unable to keep still. "We know what your lawyer friend said, and we know what Carl reported, but Quentin doesn't know that. It makes sense to let him continue staying here where we can keep an eye on him. We don't have to say anything, even to Carl. It's perfect, Maggie."

"Perfect for you. You've already admitted that you're in love with him."

Julie paused by the window and looked down at the marina. Could her decision harm her business? She'd worked her entire adult life to expand it, but she had faith in Quentin. She turned back to her friend. "That's just it, Maggie. I do love him, and I want to give him the benefit of the doubt."

"Why don't you just tell him, get it all out in the open?" Maggie pleaded.

"How would you feel if someone confronted you with accusations like that?"

Maggie's expression turned thoughtful. "Terrible, I guess. Okay, Jules, but I hope you're right about him. If he breaks your heart I won't be responsible for my actions."

The phone rang and Maggie answered it. Julie went outside and ran down the steps, glad to be away from her friend's knowing eyes. Maggie knew her too well, and it wouldn't be long until she sensed the indecision simmering right below the surface of her confident façade.

Grateful for a distraction, she pitched in and helped to clean the returned boats. The familiar work was mindless, but she took pleasure in keeping in touch with the condition of each boat, and the hours passed quickly as she worked alongside the cleaning crew.

"Hey, Julie." Maggie's niece Jenna turned off the vacuum cleaner and inspected the carpet. "Where's Quentin? We haven't seen him around today."

Julie kept her head down, hiding a smile as Cindy chimed in.

"Yeah, we think he's hot."

Cindy took a long drink from a bottle of water and looked over at Julie. "What do you think, boss? Don't you think he's easy on the eyes?"

"I guess so." Julie had moved into the kitchen and was on her knees, wiping out the oven. "He was around here a lot when I was young, so I'm used to having him around." She sat back on her heels, unaware that the subject of their discussion was standing on the dock outside the houseboat, a glint of amusement in his eyes. "But I must say when I look down here in the mornings, he gets my heart started."

"I'm flattered." His voice was like liquid heat, and it raced through her body. She gave the spotless oven one final wipe and stood up slowly. The rest of the cleaning crew had disappeared. She shook her head, embarrassed for him as much as herself. "I'll get them for that," she vowed, but her smile disproved her words. He looked wonderful standing out there in the sun, and any lingering thoughts of his association with

Delahunt flew out of her mind. She stepped onto the back deck and leaned against the railing, facing him.

"How did it go with the doctor?"

He raised his shoulders. "All right. He was straightforward, which was good."

Julie studied him. He appeared to have accepted the inevitable. "I don't know much about Alzheimer's disease myself."

"I don't think the medical profession really understands it either." His gaze slid up and down the dock, stopping briefly at the empty berths, but Julie sensed that he wasn't really seeing anything. "Doc Austen says not to expect too much and it'll get easier." He stepped from the brilliance of the dock onto the shaded back deck. The boat rocked gently and he stood with legs braced apart, eyes fixed on her mouth.

Time seemed to stand still as they looked at each other. He reached out and caressed the side of her neck, his touch whisper-light as his thumb brushed the soft underside of her jaw. Julie gripped the railing to keep her legs from buckling.

"Julie, there's something else. I—"

He stopped in mid-sentence and his head came up sharply, eyes alert as he looked over her shoulder.

She turned to see a Royal Canadian Mounted Police officer striding down the dock.

"Can I help you?" she asked, stepping out onto the dock.

"Are you Mrs. Chapman?"

Julie nodded.

"I'm Constable Reade, Mrs. Chapman. Is Nicholas Chapman your son?"

Julie's hand flew to her mouth. "Oh, my God. Is he all right? Has there been an accident?" She grabbed Quentin's arm, steadying herself.

The office glanced quickly at Quentin before settling his gaze on Julie. "No, Mrs. Chapman. Nicholas hasn't been in an accident, but we have him down at the station. He was caught shoplifting from the department store in town."

"You must be mistaken. Nicholas wouldn't shoplift anything." She looked up at Quentin for confirmation.

"I'm sorry, ma'am." The officer's expression was compassionate. "Could I ask you to come with me, please?"

"We'll follow you down to the station, Constable." Quentin's steady presence was exactly what Julie needed. His hand came to rest at her waist and she straightened, thankful for his support.

"Yes, we'll be right behind you," she said, shooting Quentin a look of thanks.

"This doesn't sound like Nick at all," she said, almost running in her haste to get to the parking lot. Quentin was forced to lengthen his stride to keep up with her. "I know most parents are in denial when their kids do something wrong, but he just wouldn't do something like that."

Quentin nodded. "I agree," he said, pausing to look from his car to hers.

"Let's take mine," she said, pulling open the door. "We'll be bringing him back home."

She slid behind the wheel and leaned back against the headrest, tears streaming down her face. She turned to him, smiling bleakly through the tears. "I don't even have my purse, or my keys. Would you mind getting them from the office?"

Quentin returned a moment later.

"What did Maggie say?" Julie asked, sliding the key into the ignition.

"She asked me what he was accused of stealing. I had to

tell her that we hadn't even asked." He looked at her sharply. "Do you want me to drive?"

"No, I'm fine." She turned on the ignition and they headed downtown.

Had Nick been behaving differently recently? Julie searched her recent memory, but there was nothing that stood out. The only change in their lives had been Quentin's arrival. She glanced over at him as they followed the police car. His influence on Nick had been positive, she was sure of that. No, it had to be something else. Lost in thought, she scarcely noticed the other vehicles on the road, and was startled to find they'd arrived at the RCMP detachment.

Quentin jumped out and came around to her door. "I want to go in with you," he said, his tone indicating that he wouldn't take no for an answer.

"I appreciate that," she said, and stepped out into the heat of the afternoon.

Quentin closed the car door but remained beside the car. He was staring across the street and Julie followed his gaze. Standing in the shade of an old cedar, Nick's friend Ryan was watching the RCMP building, a haunted expression on his face. A small youngster, he seemed to shrink even more as Quentin made eye contact.

Quentin pretended to reach for something through the open car window. "Isn't that Nick's friend Ryan over there, under the tree?"

Julie frowned and glanced across the street. "Yes, it is," she said, giving Quentin a puzzled look. "I wonder what he's doing here."

"Maybe we'll find out," he said enigmatically, and guided her up the stairs.

Nick looked up as Julie and Quentin walked into the police station. He was sitting forlornly on a plastic chair, his running shoes swinging inches above the floor. Julie's heart lurched as she looked into the large brown eyes swimming with tears.

"Thank you for coming down, Mrs. Chapman." The man behind the desk rose. "Would you step into my office please?" He was tall and well built, with a small scar on his chin. Julie was reminded of Harrison Ford.

"My name is Sergeant Burnett, and I'd like to talk to you for a moment before you see your son."

Julie swallowed and nodded.

"Your son was caught outside White's Department Store with a baseball glove." He paused to observe Julie's reaction. "He hadn't paid for it."

She turned to Quentin, and the surprise on his face mirrored her feelings. "A baseball glove? Nick? Are you sure?"

"I'm afraid so." The sergeant slid his chair forward, resting his elbows on his desk. "Mr. Fox, the store owner, said Nick was standing in front of the store looking down at the glove when he came out and caught him."

Julie shook her head in disbelief. "But Nick already has two gloves. Why would he steal another one?"

"We've tried talking to him, but he won't say anything. That's why I wanted to speak with you first. All he would tell me was his name . . . and yours, of course." The sergeant's knowing gaze slid from Julie to Quentin, then back again. "It's unusual for a child of this age to be so reluctant to talk." He smiled thinly. "Usually we can't shut them up once they're caught."

Julie sat up straighter. "What specifically would you like to know?" She surprised herself with the firmness of her voice.

"We'd like to know if he was with anyone else." The sergeant scanned a report on his desk. "Mr. Fox was quite sure that there were two youngsters in the store."

Quentin walked over to the window of the corner office and looked across the street to the park. "All right, Sergeant. We'll see what we can find out."

"Are you a member of the family?" the sergeant asked.

"No, I'm not." His eyes rested on Julie, his expression softening. "I'm a friend of the family."

"Take your time with him. And if you don't mind a word of advice, take it easy. He's pretty scared right now." The sergeant led them to an empty interview room, motioned for Nick to follow, then closed the door and left them alone.

Julie looked around at the pale yellow walls and the utilitarian table, covered with a random pattern of rings from years of coffee stains. She tossed her purse on the table and knelt down, holding out her arms. Nick was suddenly not too old for hugs, and he ran into her arms, just as he had done as a small child. He tucked his chin over her shoulder, and quiet sobs racked his body.

"I'm sorry, Mom," he said finally. "I didn't mean to hurt you." He pulled back and dabbed at his eyes with the back of his hand.

Julie held him at arm's length and looked into his young face. She brushed his hair back, struggling to find the right words.

"You haven't hurt me, Nick. If you're hurting anyone, it's yourself." She shot a quick glance at Quentin, who nodded silently. "I can't believe you did something like this. I mean, why would you take a baseball glove? You have two already." Her fingers slid down his arms and she held on to his hands, giving them a small shake. "The police want to know if there was someone with you. Can you tell me what that's about?"

Nick swallowed and looked from his mother to Quentin. "I can't," he said, his young voice quavering.

"But Nicky—" Julie closed her eyes and willed herself to remain calm. She rose from the floor and sank onto a chair. "How long have you been here? Have you had anything to eat?" The mothering instinct took over. At least she could feed her child.

"I'm okay," mumbled Nick, staring at the floor.

Quentin pushed away from the wall. "I saw a soda machine next door and I'm thirsty. Would anybody like something while I'm at it?" He looked at Nick. "How about it, sport, would you like a cold drink?"

Nick raised his head and nodded.

Quentin was back in two minutes with three cans of soda in his arms. Condensation beaded the outside of the cans and he handed one to Nick, who popped the tab and drank thirstily.

"So." Quentin's tone was conversational. "Why are you covering for Ryan?"

Nick's head snapped around and his eyes grew wide as he looked incredulously at the older man. "How did you know?"

Quentin turned to Julie with a reassuring smile, then leaned closer to Nick. "Because your mom and I saw him across the street when we came in, and he looked worried." He sat back and took a long drink from his can. "Besides, we knew you wouldn't steal anything." He tilted his head toward Julie. "Your mom particularly. She knew that all along."

Nick looked at his mother, relief written all over his face. "Did you, Mom?" He slid off his chair and ran to her, clutching her around the waist. "You're the greatest." He pulled back, his expression serious. "But if I tell them who did it, then Ryan will get in trouble. I can't let that happen." He looked desperately from Julie to Quentin.

"Because he's afraid of his father, isn't he?" Quentin's voice was low, and Julie sensed his anger.

"Yeah." Nick looked at Quentin suspiciously. "How did you know that?"

"I have a bit of experience with that myself," he said quietly.

Nick's eyes widened, and he took another drink.

Quentin leaned forward, elbows on his knees. "Also, because of what I went through as a kid, I became a member of Big Brothers. I worked with them right up until last year. I had two little brothers during that time, and they both came from abusive homes." He paused, lost in thought. "I know the signs."

"What should we do?" Nick turned to Quentin, and Julie felt a small jab of jealousy.

Quentin's eyes met hers. "Let's ask your mom what she thinks," he said smoothly. "Three heads are better than one."

"Yeah, Mom. What do you think we should do?"

"First of all, we have to tell the police the truth. We can't have them thinking that you stole anything."

"But, Mom—"

"No, Nick. Your mom's right. I've been thinking, and maybe there's a way we can sort this out without Ryan's dad finding out." He looked over Nick's head at Julie. "Would you let me talk to the sergeant first?" She nodded, her trust in him implicit.

"Great, I'll be right back." He set down his empty can.

"Do you think I'll still be able to go to camp?" Nick lined up the empty soda cans on the table.

"I don't see why not," said Julie, "as long as you promise me one thing."

"What's that?"

"You have to promise to tell me the truth in the future." Julie paused to let her words sink in. "No matter what happens. I understand what you were trying to do for your friend, and it may have seemed like the right thing at the time, but it wasn't, Nick. It wasn't right at all."

"I know that now."

"All right, then. Give me your promise."

Nick raised his head and he seemed older somehow. "I promise, Mom." He fell silent and his gaze returned to the soda cans he was rearranging on the table. "Ryan's not bad, Mom. He doesn't have a bike, or a baseball glove, or anything. I know I'm just a kid and I'm not supposed to know stuff like this, but I'm pretty sure his father drinks a lot. I always see liquor bottles near the garbage when I'm over there. And I've heard him yelling at Ryan."

Julie reached out to her son. "You know, Nicky, not all men are like your dad, or like Ryan's dad, either." She slid an arm around his waist and he leaned against her, evidence of his need for reassurance. "Most fathers love their children and treat them well. Why, look at Uncle Mike, or your grandfather."

He turned, and his dark eyes met hers. "Or Quentin. He would never yell at me."

She looked at her son for a moment, then smiled. "Or Quentin. You're right."

Nick squirmed out of her embrace but continued to stand beside her. "I wish he didn't have to leave."

Julie shot a startled look at her son. He had just spoken her innermost thoughts. "Me too, Nicky. But he lives in Vancouver, and we can't expect him to stay here forever."

The door opened and they both looked up to see Quentin and the sergeant.

"The sergeant would like to have a word with you, Nick, and then we're going home." Quentin nodded briefly at Julie and she stood up, her hand on Nick's shoulder.

"Go along then, Nick. We'll wait for you out front."

Nick looked from his mother to Quentin, then followed the sergeant into his office.

Julie and Quentin walked silently down the steps into the late afternoon sunshine. The heat from the pavement was intense, and she looked across the road to the shade of the park. "Let's wait over there," she said to Quentin, "and you can tell me what happened."

Quentin guided her across the street and they settled on a bench in sight of the front door of the police station.

"The store owner called while I was in with the sergeant. He doesn't think it was Ryan's intention to steal the glove. The boys were admiring it and kidding around. He says they went outside without realizing it." Quentin reached down and picked up a pinecone, absently picking it apart. "When Ryan realized he'd been spotted, he panicked. He handed the glove to Nick and ran off."

Somehow Julie couldn't be angry with Nick's friend. "So what's going to happen to Ryan?"

"Nothing." Quentin smiled, and her eyes were drawn to his dimple. "Nothing bad, anyway. The store owner's had a lot of losses to shoplifting, and he admits he overreacted. He got the glove back, and he says he's never had any problem with either kid." His smile faded. "The police have had a string of domestic disturbance calls at Ryan's home. Evidently his mother is too afraid to call the cops, so the neighbors do it every time they hear something going on. The RCMP are going to arrange for Ryan to get some counseling at school, and they're going to get a social worker to visit his mother. They'll be sure Ryan's father isn't around, so they can explain her options. If she decides to stay with him, there's nothing they can do about it, but they'll be keeping a closer eye on the situation."

Julie rocked back and forth on the bench as she listened to Quentin. "Maybe I should get to know her," she said, almost to herself. "Maybe I can help her see that she *can* get along without him, if that's what she chooses." Her thoughts drifted back in time. "I could tell her about my own situation, and tell her how Nick thrived after his father left." She looked up, her eyes bright. "It's worth a try."

Quentin picked up a lock of her hair and curled it around his finger. "You're an amazing woman, Jules. Is it any wonder I can't get you out of my mind?"

For a brief moment she allowed herself to dream of a future with this man.

"Hi, Mom." Nick appeared before them, looking sober.

They all walked back across the street to Julie's vehicle.

Quentin glanced at his watch. "Hey, you guys, I'm hungry. Is anyone up for a hamburger?"

Julie was grateful for the suggestion. "That's a great idea. Shall we go down by the bridge again? We're getting to be regulars there. How about you, Nick? Are you game?"

Her son's face lit up, and he began to look normal for the first time since they'd arrived at the police station.

Chapter Ten

So what did the sergeant say?" Julie's tone was gentle as she questioned Nick.

He dunked one of his French fries in gravy and looked up, his eyes solemn. "He said they aren't going to arrest Ryan or anything, but what we did was very serious. He told me what happens when you get a police record and stuff like that." He ate a few fries, unusually quiet, then turned to Quentin. "Do you think Ryan is a bad kid?"

Quentin set down his hamburger and gave his full attention to the boy. "No, Nick, I don't. Not at all. He's had a lot of tough breaks in his life." He leaned forward. "Some people who've had a rocky start like Ryan blame everybody else for whatever goes wrong in their lives, but that's a cop-out. Ryan is responsible for his own actions just the same as you are. That's the most important lesson you can both learn from this."

Julie watched her son absorb this information. She could always tell when he was really listening, because those were the times he appeared most nonchalant. The message

128

was being received loud and clear, and she knew that he would repeat it back to her in an oblique fashion sometime during the coming week.

Nick nodded and they continued eating, the tension of the afternoon blown away on the gentle breeze.

Julie smiled to herself while Nick and Quentin squabbled good-naturedly over the remaining fries. Quentin had been her rock this afternoon, and with all that had transpired, she'd completely forgotten about what Maggie had revealed earlier. Had that happened only this morning? It seemed like forever ago. She chanced another look at Quentin just as he looked up, a smile of contentment on his face. Their eyes held, and it took every ounce of strength she possessed to smile and look away.

A napkin blew off the table and Nick ran to pick it up. Julie gathered up the remains of her meal and Nick's. "Hey, kiddo. I'll bet you're ready to go home."

"Yeah, Mom. I'm kinda tired."

Julie looked at Quentin and raised her eyebrows.

"I'm ready if you are." His eyes held hers again as the words hung in the air between them. She didn't trust herself to respond.

On the drive home they were all quiet, lost in their own thoughts. Nick stared out the window, and when they pulled in beside Quentin's car he jumped out quickly. He ran up the stairs to their living quarters, stopped at the top of the steps, and looked down. "Thanks for everything, Quentin."

"You're welcome, young man." Quentin watched him go into the house, then turned to Julie. "He's a good kid, but then you've done a good job with him." He ducked under the weeping willow and walked onto the grass. "I was proud of the way he stuck up for what he thought was right."

Julie walked beside him, matching her steps to his leisurely pace. "Me too." She reached for a strand of willow. "What a day this has been," she said, running her fingers down the branch. "Did you know that this tree contains the same chemicals as in aspirin? I'm surprised I don't have a headache after all that."

They stopped by the rock wall and Quentin lifted her up to her favorite spot. He brushed the hair away from her temple with a light touch. "I'm glad you don't have a headache," he said, dropping his hand. "You've already been through a lot today."

"You don't know the half of it." The words were out before she realized it, but he didn't seem to notice. He hopped up onto the wall beside her. Looking at him still made her heart flutter. Perhaps Maggie's revelation this morning had been a bad dream.

"Hi, kiddies." Startled out of her reverie, Julie turned to see her friend coming around the old tree. "Remember me?"

Quentin jumped down, a look of consternation on his face. "Maggie, I'm sorry. I owe you an apology." He turned to Julie. "I promised Maggie one of us would call her when we found out what was going on with Nick."

"Come on, guys. You're killing me here. I thought I heard Nicky running upstairs a few minutes ago. What happened?"

"He didn't steal anything." The pressures of the day finally got to Julie, and tears started to run down her face.

"Then why are you crying?" Maggie looked at Quentin. "Why is she crying?"

"Because she's tired, I think. Everything turned out just fine, but Julie can tell you."

"You're darned right she will." Maggie grabbed her friend

by the arm. "Come on, I'll make you a cup of tea and you can tell Auntie Maggie everything."

Julie looked over her shoulder at Quentin. "I think I *will* go in. Thanks again for everything."

He lifted a hand and she allowed Maggie to lead her away.

"For crying out loud, Julie, you're making him sound like a cross between Mother Teresa and Hercule Poirot. Next you're going to tell me he can leap tall buildings in a single bound."

Julie laughed and poured herself some more tea. "Well, I am impressed. I don't think I would have figured it out myself. You know—about Ryan being the one with the glove."

"Yeah, I've got to admit, that was pretty clever." Maggie stood by the picture window in the living room, looking thoughtful. "And you say he's been in Big Brothers? Well, dammit!"

Julie watched her friend, knowing that Maggie was struggling with the same inconsistencies that had been creeping into her mind. It was getting harder and harder to believe that Quentin was in Sicamous on behalf of Delahunt Holdings. After all, they had no actual proof.

Maggie turned from the window, her brow creased by a frown. "I don't mean to rain on your parade, but let's stay cautious around him—although I admit it's becoming harder all the time." She gathered up the cups and the teapot and took them into the kitchen.

"Quentin was right, you know. You look tired, so I'm going to get out of here and let you get some rest." Maggie stopped with her hand on the door. "Oh, and your brother called. He'll be arriving tomorrow. Happy days." She wiggled her fingers and disappeared out the door.

Julie picked up a book from Nick's bed and set it on the bedside table. Her son slept soundlessly, legs tangled in his sheets. As she pulled the sheet up to his waist, she considered the pitfalls awaiting him in his teenage years, and a tendril of fear wrapped around her heart. For the first time, she wondered if she could do it on her own. Today she had allowed herself to lean on Quentin, and his presence had made the whole ordeal more bearable. The three of them had faced the problem together, and it had felt right.

She switched off Nick's light and wandered into her own bedroom, drained by the emotions of the day.

When she went into the kitchen the next morning, Nick was seated at the breakfast table in his bathing suit and a T-shirt, eating cereal and reading a book. He seemed subdued, but otherwise unaffected by yesterday's events.

"Good morning, sweetie. What's up today?"

"Nothing much. We were going to hit a few balls down at the park . . . you know, get ready for the game tonight. But that's not until this afternoon."

Julie clapped her hand to her forehead. "I must be having a senior moment. I forgot you had a game tonight."

"Come on, Mom. You're not that bad."

"Why, thank you, young man. You make me feel *soooo* much better!" She laughed and took the chair across from her son. "I wanted to ask you something, Nicky. Do you miss the picnics we used to have on the lake?"

"I guess so. I mean, when Dad was acting nice, it was

fun." He pushed his cereal bowl away. "What made you ask that?"

"Well, Uncle Mike and your cousins are coming today, and your grandma and granddad arrive tomorrow, so I was thinking we could all go for a picnic somewhere on the lake. Get away from here for a while and roast some marshmallows."

Nick's wide smile telegraphed his enthusiasm. "Could we take the skis? I think maybe I could get up on skis this year."

Julie chuckled. "We'll have to get them out and dust them off. Make sure to check with Uncle Mike when he gets here, okay? We have a lot of arrivals today, so I'm going to be busy."

"For sure." Nick closed his book and jumped up, suddenly full of energy. "I'm going to go down and visit Quentin."

Julie wished it could be that simple for her. She'd like to visit Quentin too.

What would I say? she asked herself. *Would I ask him to tell me the truth about why he came here this summer, or do I even want to hear the truth? Perhaps I could just watch him work. I could watch the way his eyes darken when he's concentrating. Or the way the muscles in his arms ripple and harden as he changes a propane tank. Or I could stop acting like a lovesick schoolgirl and get on with my day.*

"Carl must have his cell phone turned off." Maggie was already in the office when Julie arrived. "Could you run down and see what's up? I'd do it myself, but the renters out on *Widgeon* want an extension, and I have to see if I can juggle things around."

"Sure." Julie glanced outside. "I wanted to see Quentin anyway."

"Well, of course you do." Maggie raised an eyebrow, then smiled and turned to her computer.

Quentin looked up as Julie came abreast of the boat he was working on. "Good morning, Boss Lady." He was kneeling on the rear deck with the hatch cover off, checking the hydraulic lines. "I saw Nick earlier and he seems recovered from yesterday's adventure." He held up a hand to shield his eyes from the sun. "And you," he said softly. "How are you?"

"I'm fine." She took a step closer. "Sorry I ran off last night."

"Me too." He rose slowly, but his eyes never left hers.

She thought he was going to reach out and gather her in his arms—right here, on the dock—and she would have gone, willingly and joyfully. But a group of renters materialized, seemingly out of nowhere, and the moment passed.

"Just thought I'd let you know Mike and his family are arriving today. I'm planning a family picnic tomorrow night when Mom and Dad are here. You're invited, of course. After all, you're practically family."

"I'll be there." He stepped out onto the dock. "Is there anything I can do?"

"Oh, no. I can manage." She paused. "Wait a minute. Nick wants to learn to water ski, so if you could give him a few pointers, I'd appreciate it."

"That would be a pleasure, but what about the picnic?" He flashed her a boyish smile. "After all, I'm a fair cook, and not afraid to admit it."

"So I hear." She stepped closer to him to let a departing

group pass. "You really have to stop being so modest, or we'll never learn how great you are."

A fully loaded cart rolled by and he reached out to steady her. His touch sent a shimmering sensation dancing across her skin. "Don't worry," he said, his voice low and intimate. "I intend to make sure you find out."

Julie walked away, her heart racing. She felt his eyes on her, and her skin burned from the heat of his gaze. She glanced back.

"You look good today, Squirt," he said, and she made herself keep going, afraid that he might see into her heart. It wasn't until she was walking up the stairs to the office that she realized she'd forgotten to look for Carl.

"Do you mind if I take off for a couple of hours?" Quentin asked Carl, who was fiddling with the controls on a hot tub. "Everything is serviced, and I'll be back in time to help with the new arrivals."

"No problem. What with our staff being back to full strength, and with your help, I've never had it so good." The maintenance supervisor wasn't surprised by the request. He'd heard Nick ask for another swimming lesson. Sure enough, Quentin headed toward *Chickadee*, where Nick lay on the dock with his head over the side, watching for fish. Personally, Carl was pleased to see him giving the kid so much attention, but he worried about the letdown when Quentin went back to the coast.

He took a moment to watch the two of them together. Things had changed since Quentin's arrival. Julie was obviously besotted with him, Nick idolized him, and the whole operation was running smoothly. Even Apex Houseboats had stopped upsetting Julie with their overtures to the staff and, as far as he knew, with their offers to buy the place. He smiled to himself as Quentin and Nick headed toward the parking lot, Nick chattering away six to the dozen.

"I'm getting better, don't you think?"

Quentin tried not to smile. The youngster had natural ability, and his need for approval tugged at his heart. "You bet," he said, and Nick launched himself off the bottom, long even strokes pulling him through the water. "That's right, slow it down a bit and feel yourself move through the water. Your kick is much stronger. I'm proud of you."

Nick swam past, his legs churning the surface of the lake, and Quentin wiped his face with the towel around his neck. He'd been standing in the water for half an hour and was starting to get cold. "Let's swim out to the float and warm up in the sun." He tossed his towel toward the beach.

"I'm not cold, but okay." Nick's teeth had been chattering for several minutes, and Quentin hid another smile. He'd been the same when he was young. There was never enough time to be in or on the water. He swam toward the float, allowing Nick to catch up with him. The fiberglass surface was hot to the touch, and it felt good as he hauled himself up. Nick copied his position, feet in the water and arms propped at his sides, looking back toward the shore.

"I haven't seen your uncle Mike in ages." He shot a sideways glance at Nick. "Since before you were born." He eased himself back and lay down with his hands behind his head, looking up at the sky. "He went up north, and I ended up in Vancouver."

The heat from the float loosened his muscles, and his thoughts drifted. How had he ended up so far removed from what really mattered? It was no wonder he was willing to give it up so easily. He didn't regret the hard work to get his degrees, or the effort of building a successful business. That was all part of what had brought him to this moment. Knowing that he was respected and successful was gratifying, but it didn't add up to much when weighed against what really counted: family, peace of mind, and making a living doing something you truly enjoyed. To him, those things represented the brass ring—and he wanted it more than he'd wanted anything in his life.

"Mom says you have to go back." Nick's voice broke into his thoughts. The youngster's expression was fierce, challenging him to deny it.

Quentin sat up and turned to face Nick squarely. "For a while, at least. But I'll be back."

Nick looked at him as if trying to assess the truth of what he had heard. "My dad went away, and he never came back."

"Well, then." Quentin tried to keep his voice light, but it was difficult. "He's a foolish man."

"How come?"

"Because he hasn't been around to see what a great swimmer you've become." Quentin gave him a gentle punch on the arm, then turned it into a quick, brief hug. "Not to mention a fantastic baseball player." He paused while his words sunk in. "I'm not like your dad, Nick. When I say I'm coming back, I mean it."

Nick's face was transformed by a radiant smile. "Really?"

"Absolutely." Quentin's heart lightened when he saw the joy on Nick's face. "I promise."

Quentin took a detour on the way home and pulled into a parking space across the street from White's Department Store. Nick eyed it nervously.

"I have some business to do, Nick. Would you mind playing some video games for a while?" Personally, Quentin detested the idea of kids hanging around video gaming parlors when they should be outside, but he wanted to disappear by himself for a few minutes. He pulled a couple of dollars out of his pocket. "This is all the small change I've got, so make it last, okay?"

He returned twenty minutes later to find Nick fully engrossed in a pinball game. "Good score, my man. I was never very good at this sort of thing myself."

"Oh." Nick glanced up. "Did they have pinball games back in the old days?"

Quentin gave him a gentle cuff and they both laughed. "Good one, sport. Come on, let's go home." They drove back to SunBird, discussing the various types of pinball machines.

Julie looked up as Nick bounded into the office, a beach towel around his neck. "What time is Uncle Mike getting here?"

"Nick, have you been swimming? I told you to let me know where you're going." Julie's tone conveyed her displeasure.

"But I was with Quentin. He gave me another swimming lesson." Nick looked down at his feet. "Carl knew where we were."

"That doesn't matter. I'm your mother, Nick, and I want to know where you go." Julie knew that part of her anger stemmed from her own guilt at not spending more time with her son. As for the other reason . . . well, she didn't have time to think about that right now. She took a deep breath. "Your uncle Mike will be here any time. He said somewhere around three."

"Okay, Mom." He frowned, unaccustomed to dealing with angry outbursts. "Do I have to wait around?" He took a few tentative steps toward the door. "Us guys were going to meet at the ballpark."

"Yes. No." Julie fluttered a hand in his direction. "You don't have to wait, Nicky. I'll tell Jeremy where you are when he gets here."

Mike's son, Jeremy, was three years older than Nick, but the two had always hit it off. Mike's daughter, Nicole, was a small and studious version of her mother. The two children were a pleasure to have around, and Julie looked forward to seeing them again.

Maggie looked up as Nick ran off, then returned her attention to her computer screen.

"I guess I overreacted, huh?"

Her friend looked up, her expression blank. "Did I say anything?"

"You don't have to say anything, Mags. I can tell by the set of your shoulders."

Maggie made a few keystrokes and the printer started to spit out paper. "Listen, kiddo. You're uptight. I understand that. But don't take it out on Nick, okay?"

Things must be bad for Maggie to speak out about Nick. They discussed everything, but Maggie never, ever commented on the way she handled her son. She massaged the back of her neck. "You're right. You know, I almost wish he would go back home now. Then maybe things would get back to normal around here."

"Hi, sis!" Mike lifted her off the ground in a bear hug. "Boy, it's good to see you."

Julie stood back and looked at him fondly. Mike had

inherited their father's dark, curly hair, his height, and his unflagging good humor.

Mike turned his hazel eyes on Maggie. "Maggie Mine, you get better looking every time I see you."

"You know it!" Maggie winked at him. "And you're not hard on the eyes yourself."

They laughed together. Their mutual teasing had started years before, and reunions weren't complete without the familiar exchange. Sharon stood in the doorway, shaking her head.

"I'm glad to see nothing's changed. Hi, Maggie." She gave her a quick peck on the cheek, then walked over and hugged Julie. "Good to see you again, Julie."

"Where are the kids?" Julie looked behind her sister-in-law.

"Oh, you know them. They headed straight for the dock." She wandered over to the window. "There they are, pestering Carl." She stopped in mid-stride. "Whoa! Who is that?" She turned to Julie. "Is that Quentin? I didn't realize he was so . . ." At a loss for words, she looked back down at the dock. "So gorgeous."

Mike spotted Quentin at the same time, and a boyish grin shaved years from his face. "There he is!" He strode out the door without noticing Julie's discomfort and was soon on the dock, slapping his friend on the back.

The women watched as the men hugged, oblivious to the customers flowing around them. Faces wreathed in smiles, they chatted animatedly, broad gestures punctuating their words.

Sharon was the first to speak. "When Mike said his old school chum would be here, I didn't think much about it." She turned to Julie. "He's talked about Quentin a lot over the years, but the only pictures we have show a couple of gangly kids in a sailboat. Good lord, Julie, how do you keep your hands off him?"

"It's not easy." Julie managed a weak smile. "He's sure got something, doesn't he?" Her eyes flickered over to Maggie, who sat with both hands clutched around her neck, a signal that she was holding back one of her pithy remarks. "Come on down, I'll introduce you." She guided Sharon toward the door and stopped to give Maggie a small pinch on the arm. "Maggie can take care of the office." She glared at her friend, and Maggie stuck out her tongue in return. Julie led Sharon downstairs with a smile on her face.

Chapter Eleven

Quentin saw them coming and grasped Mike's arm, turning him toward the women. "Introduce me to this beautiful young thing who must have been out of her mind to marry an old scalawag like you."

Mike performed the introductions and Quentin charmed Sharon completely. Julie was proud of the way he smoothly made her sister-in-law feel as though she'd always been part of their group, and she smiled her thanks at him.

Quentin's pager beeped three times, a signal that a party was waiting for assistance at the office. "I'd better go and help the new arrivals," he said, looking up toward the office.

"Hey, you guys have a business to run here, and we're crowding the dock." Mike looked around. "Looks like things are going well, Jules. Way to go." He caught up with Quentin and they strode together to the parking lot. "What's up tonight? Can we get caught up then?"

"I promised to visit my dad tonight, then I promised to

catch the last half of Nick's ball game. How about we meet after that?"

"Perfect. See you then."

"Can I help get dinner ready or something?" Sharon looked around at the orderly kitchen. "I've never quite figured out how you manage to run a business and a house and be a single mother—all at the same time!"

"Easy—I don't think about it." Julie took a bowl of cooked potatoes from the fridge. "I could use some help with the potato salad, though. Nick has an early ball game." She stuck her head in the fridge again. "I wasn't going to do anything fancy for tonight. Potato salad, green salad, sliced tomatoes, sliced ham, and some rolls. That should just about do it. Your kids eat all that stuff, don't they?"

Sharon laughed. "My kids eat anything." She grabbed a knife. "Same bedrooms as before?"

Julie nodded and glanced at her watch. "Two more arrivals and we're finished for the day. You know where to find anything you need, right?" Sharon nodded. "Good, then I'll go back down to help with the check-ins. We just might eat and make it to the ball game on time, thanks to you."

Quentin showed up at the end of the fifth inning and parked his car well away from any stray baseballs. Julie spotted him immediately and watched him thread his way through the onlookers. He wore beautifully tailored slacks and a pale blue shirt with the arms rolled up. She loved the way he moved, and her heart caught in her throat as she recalled the way he looked in shorts and a T-shirt. Either way, he was compellingly masculine. He paused, searching the diamond for Nick, and the young boy's eyes lit up at the sight of him.

"Hey, pal. I saved you a seat." Mike stood up and waved his friend toward the end of the bleachers, away from Julie and Sharon. Quentin paused and scanned the bleachers until he spotted Julie, and his eyes softened for a moment before Mike pulled him up into the stands.

"What was he like as a teenager?" asked Sharon, an amused smile on her lips.

"Who, Mike?" Julie gave her an innocent look.

"Yeah, right." Sharon chuckled softly. "Julie, a blind man on a galloping horse can see that you and Quentin can't take your eyes off one another."

"Really?" That infuriating blush was giving her away again. "To answer your question, he had a tough childhood. Even so, if you asked him, I think he'd tell you that it made him what he is today."

"And what is that?"

Julie looked away. "I was referring to his business expertise. He's quite successful."

Sharon gave her a gentle bump with her shoulder. "Did you guys, you know, get together when you were young?"

"Just once." Julie sighed and told her the story of her graduation night. "And then he went away and I never saw him again, until a few days ago."

"And he's going back? That's hard to believe."

"Why?" Julie asked anxiously. "Why do you say that?"

"Well, for one thing, the air practically sizzles when you look at each other. And for another, Nick is crazy about him. So what are you going to do about it?"

Julie watched her son field a ball, then look to the

stands for approval. Quentin and Mike were on their feet, cheering.

"I don't know, Sharon. I really don't know."

The game was decided when Ryan caught a fly ball, retiring the opposite side. The adults watched indulgently as Nick's team celebrated their first win.

"Hey, Mom! Guess what? Ryan got a new glove." Nick looked from Julie to Quentin, eyes shining. "Coach says someone animously donated a glove for anyone who doesn't own one. Cool, huh?"

Julie laughed. "You mean *anonymously*." She smiled at Ryan, who stood proudly, tossing a ball into his new glove. The youngster beamed with confidence and her heart went out to him. She looked around for Quentin, but Mike had cornered him by the edge of the stands. Her brother hadn't stopped talking since he arrived, but Quentin listened patiently, a smile lurking around the corners of his mouth.

She turned to Sharon. "It usually takes a while for the kids to slow down after a game. Want to walk over to the bandstand while the kids go for ice cream? It's too early to go home, and I've told Nick where to find us."

"I'd like that." Sharon handed her children some money and the two women wandered toward the park. The sun had disappeared behind the hills, but the air was soft and warm, carrying the scent of roses from the city's well-tended gardens. The volunteer band, comprised of some surprisingly talented local musicians, had started their first set, and the music beckoned them with the familiar strains of a Cole Porter melody.

Julie motioned to a knoll overlooking the bandstand. "Let's

sit over there. The kids will be able to spot us when they come back. She lowered herself onto the grass and rotated her shoulders, sighing deeply. The musicians launched into "I've Got You Under My Skin," and Julie hummed along.

Sharon sank down beside her and fussed around for a few moments before finally speaking. "Are you in love with him, Julie?"

Julie gave her a lopsided smile. "Sometimes I think I've been in love with him all my life, but that's the easy answer, isn't it?" She plucked at a patch of clover, gathering her thoughts. "When he walked onto the dock last week, I felt like I was the one who'd come home, not him." She tilted her head and peered at Sharon. "Do you know what I mean? It was as though I had finally found the missing piece of the puzzle, and it had been in my hand all along." She paused. "When I'm with him, I feel complete. He . . ." She placed a hand on her chest, her fingers fluttering. "He takes my breath away, Sharon, corny as that may sound. And when I see him again, after even a short separation, my heart starts pounding like it wants to jump out of my chest."

Sharon's eyes softened. "How does *he* feel? I mean, I know how he looks at you, but has he said anything?"

"We haven't gotten that far yet." She lowered her eyes. "He just found out a few days ago that his father has Alzheimer's. It's a long, sad story, but he was really knocked for a loop."

Sharon reached out and placed a hand on Julie's knee. "I'm sorry, Julie, but it'll work out. If I've ever seen two people who were meant to be together, it's you two."

Julie looked up. "Thanks, Sharon." Her attention was diverted by the children traipsing across the grass. "So much for our quiet moment. Here they come."

* * *

"Thanks for agreeing to come here." Quentin glanced around the diner. "As I was saying, I visited my father, but I couldn't bring myself to eat there."

"That's okay." Mike waved to the server, indicating they'd like more coffee. "Seems like old times, to come here again."

"It does, doesn't it? I was telling Nick just this morning how long it's been since we've seen each other." Quentin regarded his friend fondly. "How did we ever let that much time go by without at least a visit?"

"Well, you never got to Williams Lake."

"And you never made it to Vancouver." Quentin shook his head. "At least we kept in touch with Christmas cards."

"Yeah." Mike toyed with his mug. "Speaking of the coast, what exactly are you *doing* up here this summer? How did you ever manage to get this much time away from work?"

Quentin laughed. "It took a lot of careful planning. What I am, basically, is a freelance contractor, so I timed my projects to give me this month off. I had to work like mad to finish the reports for my last few assignments, but I got them done, and here I am."

He took a sip of coffee. "But the answer to your question is a bit more complicated. I've been taking a second look at the type of work I've been doing, and it's time for a change." He leaned forward. "I went to a seminar last year, and one of the speakers said something that really made me think. The gist of his message was that when you stop enjoying your work, get out. I know it's not that simple for most people, but it was as though he was talking to me, as though he could see inside my head. So I planned for a month off, and somehow I just gravitated here." He looked evenly at his friend. "Julie was kind enough to let me stay in one of the houseboats in exchange for helping out."

Mike's eyes narrowed. "Have you decided about the job?"

"Secret?" Quentin held up his hand, little finger crooked.

Mike hooked his little finger through his friend's and they squeezed, eyes laughing as they recalled their boyhood pacts. "Secret."

"I've decided to give it up."

"Wow." Mike raised his shoulders. "What will you do?"

"I'm not quite sure yet. But I promise to keep you up to date."

"You do that." Mike stirred sugar into his coffee, his eyes thoughtful. "Julie seems to be doing well, wouldn't you say?"

Quentin shot him an oblique look. Mike didn't have a devious bone in his body. "She's turned into a beautiful woman," he said.

Mike nodded agreement. "She has, hasn't she? Well, we've had a long day, so I'd better get back and help get the kids settled down. Are you coming on the picnic tomorrow?"

Quentin grinned. "Wouldn't miss it."

"Don't be ridiculous." Maggie was at her imperious best. "Of course you're going to take the afternoon off. It's not every day your mom and dad come to visit." Maggie made shooing motions toward the door. "We only have two arrivals this afternoon, and I can handle them with one hand tied behind my back."

Julie knew better than to argue with her stubborn friend. Besides, she needed some quiet time. "Where is everybody? I've hardly seen Mom and Dad since they arrived and set up their camper."

"Your mom and Sharon have gone shopping and the kids went with them. Your dad and Mike have gone to the mill to see that new piece of equipment they installed."

"Well, in that case, I think I'll organize some stuff for the picnic." Julie hesitated, her hand on the doorframe. "Thanks, Maggie. I don't tell you that often enough, I'm afraid."

Maggie herded her through the door. "Cut that out." The lights on her console started to blink and she rolled her eyes, put a smile in her voice, and answered the phone.

Julie stood in her kitchen for a moment, organizing her thoughts. There were plenty of hot dogs for the kids, but Sharon preferred a vegetarian diet, and she wanted to make a selection of salads. She tied her hair back with a ribbon and tuned the radio to an oldies station, content to be alone for the first time in days.

She thought back to her conversation with Sharon last night. It must have been the stress of the past few days that had made her uncharacteristically forthcoming. But it had felt good to articulate her feelings for Quentin, and her sister-in-law had been a reliable sounding board. Lost in thought, she didn't notice the figure approaching the back door.

"Hiya, Squirt."

She stilled at the sound of his voice. "Hi, yourself."

He opened the screen door and she clutched at the counter to keep herself from walking into his arms. She picked up a bunch of radishes and started scrubbing them.

He walked up beside her and surveyed the ingredients spread out over the counter. "I think that's enough."

"I want to make several salads."

"No, I mean those." He pointed to the radishes.

She looked down. She'd scrubbed them so long the color was almost gone. "Oh." She was acting like a lovesick teenager, but she couldn't help it.

"I came to give you a hand." He held up his hands and she looked at them, unwilling to meet his eyes.

"Thanks, I could use some help." She inhaled slowly, calming her nerves. "How are you at chopping?"

"I think I can manage that."

"Okay, then. I'm going to make a Thai noodle salad for Sharon. If you could shred the cabbage and the carrots, I'll dig out the peppers and the rest of the stuff." She was regaining her equilibrium. "I'll boil the pasta and make the sauce."

Quentin started shredding and dicing, his movements sure and efficient. "I like this salad. I hope we're making lots."

"Do you?" Julie realized there was a lot she didn't know about Quentin. "What else do you like?"

"My tastes are eclectic." He raised an eyebrow and flashed her a rakish grin. "In food, that is. When it comes to women, I'm very predictable."

He had stopped working to look at her, and Julie pointed at the chopping board. "No slacking." She dumped the pasta into boiling water. "Is that a good thing? Predictability?" She pulled out a bowl and started to measure the ingredients for the sauce.

"It is from where I'm standing." He reached for the cilantro and her throat tightened as his arm brushed hers. "I don't enjoy playing the field."

Julie couldn't control the blush that crept into her face. "Whereas I, on the other hand, haven't even had the opportunity." She slanted a glance in his direction. "But I guess I already told you that."

He nodded. "Yes, I remember." He scooped the cut-up pieces into the bowl. "I remember everything you tell me, Julie."

"Then I'll have to be careful what I say around you."

"Yes, you will." His eyes glinted with amusement. "Now, what's next?"

For a moment she didn't know what he meant. "Oh, ah . . . could you help me drain this?" She moved to the stove. "The colander's in the sink."

Quentin tipped the pot and Julie cooled the steaming pasta with cold water.

"Chicken salad is next. You'll find the cooked chicken in the fridge." She tossed the Thai salad, then took her place beside him at the chopping board. "That was you, wasn't it?"

"What?" He looked at her indulgently, and she bumped him with her hip.

"You know. You bought the baseball glove, didn't you?"

"Now, why would you think a thing like that?" He continued chopping.

"Oh, I don't know." She bumped him again, trying to goad him into answering.

He tossed down the knife. "Don't do that, Julie." His eyes darkened. "I'm warning you."

"Or what?"

"Or this." He grabbed her around the waist and pulled her into an embrace. He looked into her eyes and a small groan escaped his lips as he brought his mouth down on hers.

This is where you were meant to be, said a voice in her head. *Right here, in this man's arms*. She melted against him, losing herself in the pleasure of his kiss.

"Ah, Julie," he said, stepping back and looking into her eyes. "I know what we agreed, but I couldn't resist. I've been thinking, and—" His head snapped up at the sound of voices. "What is it with your family? Every time I get you alone someone— Oh, hello Mrs. Sanderson."

"Quentin, is that really you?" Julie's mother set down some grocery bags and advanced, giving him a hug. "How long has it been? How are you?"

"Too long, Mrs. Sanderson, and I'm fine. How are you?"

Julie unpacked the groceries while Quentin and her mom got caught up. Sharon helped put things away, a knowing smile on her face.

"Well, I'm off to have a quick visit with Carl, and to make sure my grandchildren aren't getting in the way. It looks like everything is in control here."

The local radio station was playing a Nat King Cole song and Sharon turned it up. "His voice is so dreamy," she said, swaying to the music with her eyes closed. "It makes you believe that love can conquer all, doesn't it?"

"I hope so," murmured Julie. She looked up to find Quentin watching her intently. "I really hope so."

Joan and Bert Sanderson sat side by side, waving to people they knew as Mike guided the boat out of the Narrows.

"Do you miss it, Mom? How about you, Dad? Do you miss the business?"

Julie's father's arm tightened around her mother's shoulder and Julie smiled at the show of affection. "I sometimes miss the sounds of the lake," he said. "That sucking sound when the water hits the underside of the dock, or the peaceful sound it makes lapping against a rocky shoreline." He scanned the distant hills. "Or the throaty warble of a loon, calling to its mate. But I don't miss the work one bit. Your mom and I are too busy."

"Your father's right, you know. We have the ocean of course, but it isn't quite the same as being on the lake." Joan leaned into her husband. "That's what's so great about you carrying on the business. We can always come and visit."

"Did you have a picnic site picked out?" Mike turned around, his hair tousled by the wind.

"Anywhere there's a beach for swimming and a place to light a fire," replied Julie. "I'll leave it up to you." She glanced behind them to check on the smaller boat being towed behind. It was packed with food, skis, folding chairs and firewood. The afternoon sun was warm on her skin, and she felt carefree and happy for the first time in several days.

"Hey, Mom. Did you see me? I stood up on the water skis!" Nick loomed over her, blocking out the sun. Droplets of water sparkled on the tips of his hair, then splashed down onto her bare skin. She sat up, confused and groggy. "I'm sorry, sweetie. I fell asleep."

"That's okay." Nick pointed to the powerboat, where Quentin was doing lookout duty as Mike drove. "Quentin says I can go out again later." He flung a towel around his shoulders and ran back down to the water, where he stood with his cousin Nicole as Jeremy skied past, unprying his fingers from the tow bar to wave at his mother.

Sharon waved back, then sat down beside Julie. "Have a good sleep?"

Julie rubbed her eyes. "I suppose so, but I missed seeing Nicky get up on skis for the first time." She was almost in tears. "What kind of a mother am I, anyway?"

"You're a great mother. What you *are* is exhausted." Sharon watched as the towboat came around again. "You need a partner in that business so you can do something besides work every day." Sharon pressed her fingers to her mouth. "I'm sorry. That's none of my business. Mike hates it when I speak without thinking."

Julie gave her sister-in-law a bleak smile. "It's the truth, and I know it. You know, when Quentin first showed up I gave him this long lecture about how I could take care of myself." She picked up a handful of sand and watched it run through her fingers. "I'd talked myself into believing that I could do it all on my own, whereas right now I can think of nothing I'd like better than to have a partner. I have Maggie, of course, but she's made it clear that she doesn't want to be a business owner."

"Huh. She's been with you forever."

"That's right, but she inherited some money a couple of years ago when her grandmother passed away. I asked her then if she wanted to purchase part of the company, but she said no. It surprised me at the time, but when I thought about it, I had to admire her. She wants to get married someday, and she doesn't want the burden of owning part of a business."

"Some people are more comfortable working for someone else. Look at your brother."

Julie nodded her agreement. "Yeah, he wanted nothing to do with the business when Mom and Dad retired. And look at him—he certainly seems happy."

"He is." Sharon spoke with a certainty that Julie envied. "But I know what you mean about wanting a partner. Mike and I talk everything over." The two men pulled the boat up on shore, assisted by Nick, and Sharon chucked. "Quentin's good with the kids, isn't he?"

Julie picked up another handful of sand and tilted her palm, watching it catch the light. "He did the most amazing thing." She told Sharon about the incident with Ryan and the police. "And I'm quite sure he was the one who donated the baseball glove, although he won't admit it." She watched Quentin frolicking in the water with Nick and Jeremy, her heart in her throat. "Sometimes I think he's too good to be true."

Sharon frowned. "Perhaps. But until he proves otherwise, why not enjoy it?"

Julie bit her bottom lip. "Yeah," she whispered. "Why not?"

Chapter Twelve

Now, you're sure you have everything?" Julie peered anxiously at Nick's knapsack as they waited for Tommy's dad to pick him up. "Have you got your money safely put away?"

"Yes, Mom." Nick was showing remarkable restraint. "We checked a few minutes ago, remember?" He looked at his grandparents. "Will you still be here when I get back from camp?"

Joan tousled his hair, and he managed not to pull back. "We're leaving this morning too. But we'll probably stop in on our way back from the Calgary Stampede. If not, there's always next year."

"Okay, then." Nick's attention was diverted by the arrival of his friends. Two eager faces looked out the window and Julie smiled at the thought of the three of them going off on an adventure together.

Bruce loaded the knapsack into the rear of his SUV and Nick jumped into the back seat, then leaned out the window. "Tell Quentin I said good-bye, okay, Mom?"

"Hey, Nick. Good luck on your swimming." Quentin

appeared out of nowhere and stopped beside Julie, hands in his back pockets. "Have fun, okay?"

The youngster beamed his pleasure, gave one last wave, then turned to his friends. Quentin watched him go, then wandered back to the dock, deep in conversation with Julie's mom.

A ripple of unease crept down Julie's spine as the SUV pulled away. How was Nick going to react when Quentin went back to Vancouver, to his business? He may have been her white knight many years ago, but common sense told her it was time to let go of the dream. She wasn't prepared to risk disappointing her son a second time. She gave her head a brisk shake and entered the office.

"So, Nicky's off to camp." Maggie was pouring herself a cup of coffee. "It'll be quiet around here with him gone. You two lovebirds will have some time alone."

"I don't know, Maggie." Julie wandered over to the window. "Nick's getting so attached to him."

"And you're not?"

"Yeah, well . . ." She was distracted by the sight of Quentin deep in discussion with Carl. "I can handle it, but I don't want Nicky hurt again."

"I know you don't, Jules. Hey, here's your mom and dad."

"We just popped in to say good-bye." Julie looked up to see her mother at the door.

"I'm sorry. I don't know where the time goes." Julie hugged both of her parents and walked with them to their RV. Within moments they were on their way, and she walked slowly back to the office.

Maggie was on the phone when Julie reentered the office, and she stopped for a moment to look at her friend. She sometimes worried that she took Maggie for granted. They'd worked together for so long they could almost read each other's minds.

"Why don't you take the afternoon off," she said now. "You covered a lot for me the past few days. I think I can still remember how to use the radiophone and take reservations."

"Really? I'd love to get my hair done this afternoon." She reached for the phone, spoke, then turned to Julie. "They can take me in half an hour, if that's all right with you."

"Of course." She looked at her friend curiously. "Big date tonight?"

Maggie blushed. "I'm not sure. I just met him the other night." She fussed around with some papers on her desk. "These are the contracts for the two arrivals."

Julie ignored the paperwork. "So who is he? Do I know him?"

"He works at the mill. He's new in town." Maggie gathered her things and dashed for the door. "I'll fill you in tomorrow, okay?"

Julie followed her friend to the door and called after her as she headed for the parking lot. "Okay, but I'll expect a full report, Maggie Carlson."

She closed the door, lost in thought. She was hurt that Maggie hadn't confided in her, but in all fairness to her friend, she hadn't been around much. She'd allowed her obsession with Quentin to color her whole life. The phone rang and she settled at Maggie's desk, putting aside the disturbing thoughts as she slipped into the familiar routine.

"SunBird central, this is *Osprey*." Julie was working on the computer when the radio crackled to life.

"*Osprey*, this is SunBird. May I help you?" Julie scanned the status board as she answered, noting that *Osprey* had been out for one day. The boat was booked for a weekly rental, and the party was made up of two adults and three children.

"SunBird, we're presently at the far end of Shuswap Lake, at Scotch Creek." The male voice sounded tense, and Julie was immediately alert. This was no casual query. "I've just had a call on my cell, and we have a family emergency back in Idaho." The caller paused, and the line went dead for a moment. "Sorry, SunBird, I was just talking to my wife. Anyway, we have a family emergency. Is there any way you could come and get us? I estimate it would take something like eight hours to bring the houseboat back, and I can't wait that long." His voice cracked.

Julie didn't hesitate. Emergencies of this sort were rare, but when they happened, the staff was trained to act quickly to avoid as much stress as possible.

"*Osprey*, we can send a boat for you right away. Pack up your gear and we'll be there in about an hour."

"Thank you, SunBird."

Julie ran down to the dock.

"I'll be happy to get them," volunteered Quentin. "Carl and the boys are tied up with maintenance right now, and I've just finished *Mallard*."

Within minutes, Quentin was out of sight. *Blue Streak* would reach them within the hour, but the renter was correct. It would take a long time to bring back the houseboat.

The last booking of the day arrived and pulled out just as Quentin returned with the renters from *Osprey*. Carl and his crew assisted them to their vehicle and they were on their way to the airport within minutes.

"Did they say what the emergency was?" Julie stood beside Quentin as they pulled out.

"His brother was in an industrial accident, and they're not sure if he's going to make it. He was on the phone the whole way back, chartering an aircraft out of Vernon and keeping in touch with his family. I feel sorry for him." He handed Julie the keys. "He had the presence of mind to lock up the boat, but someone should pick it up tonight."

"Would you do it?" She held up the keys.

"Yes, I will." His fingers brushed against hers. "Will you come with me?"

All of her good intentions drifted away on the warm summer air. "I'd like that," she said. "Just give me some time to close up the office."

"I know what I'm getting into," she rationalized, muttering to herself as she switched over the phones. "Besides, maybe he'll tell me what his plans are."

It sounded convincing. So why didn't she believe it?

Quentin had just finished refueling *Streak* when Julie arrived on the dock. He held her hand as she stepped into the boat and settled herself in the left-hand seat. He kept his eyes straight ahead, not speaking as he navigated out into the lake.

She studied his profile. Why didn't she tell him how she felt about him? Why was she torturing herself, riding a constant rollercoaster of emotions?

No. She looked away. If he rejected her—confirmed her worst fears—it would all be over. For now—just for tonight— she'd drift along, pretending he felt the same.

You're only kidding yourself. Maggie's voice filled her head.

I know, she replied silently. *But it's a chance I'm willing to take.*

"Penny for your thoughts." Quentin's voice was low and

intimate. The tiny hairs on the back of her neck stood up. It was a good thing he couldn't read minds.

"They're not even worth that much," she said, keeping her tone light.

"Come on, tell me."

"Maybe later," she said, gesturing ahead. "It looks like we're here."

The houseboat was up on the shore, its lines firmly anchored with stakes in the sand. They worked efficiently together to pull the anchors and within minutes they were under way, with the runabout tied to the back.

"They had a nice spot here," she said, looking back as they pulled away from the shore. "Too bad we have to go back."

"I agree," he said with a reluctant smile. "Maybe another time?"

Would there be another time? Her heart beat faster at the thought.

"It's going to take a while to get back." He gestured to the top deck. "I'd rather drive from up there. Come on and keep me company."

Houseboats dotted both shores, pulled up for the night. Most had campfires going, and voices floated across the water, families and friends enjoying the warmth of the summer evening.

Quentin settled into the captain's chair and Julie stood beside him, enjoying the enforced leisure. Swallows skimmed the surface of the water, catching bugs in the last light of the day. On the far shore, she spotted a large cluster of branches in a dying tree and, as she pointed, an osprey swooped up to the nest with a fish in its talons. Its mate accepted the offering, its white head barely visible in the nest.

"How could I ever have left all this?" Quentin's voice held a touch of awe.

"Vancouver's a beautiful city." Julie watched for his reaction.

"Yes, but these days that doesn't seem like enough." He studied the hills, which folded in on each other, then faded into the distance. "This country is in my blood, I guess." He reached out a hand and she took it, surprised by the warmth of his skin. "And so are you." He tugged gently, pulling her to his side. He steered the boat with one hand, while the other arm encircled her waist, holding her close. "I wish it could always be like this," he said softly, and she closed her eyes, allowing herself to dream.

The night cooled and they went below. Quentin tucked her into a big chair with a quilt while he navigated from the lower position. Several hours later she awoke to pale dawn light and the ghostly shape of the railway bridge. They were almost home. As they slowed for the Narrows, an Apex houseboat passed them, and Julie looked at it thoughtfully.

"Do you want to hear something funny?" she said, rubbing the sleep from her eyes. "Last week we had a renter who told us that you work for Delahunt. Isn't that ridiculous?"

His movements stilled and her heart lodged in her throat. Why wasn't he responding? She laughed, but the sound was dry and brittle, even to her own ears. "He said you help them with their takeover bids." She should stop, but it was too late. She had to know. "Let's see, what did he call you? Oh yes, he said you're their ace in the hole."

She waited for him to deny it. "Quentin?" Her voice quaked.

He turned to her and she was struck by his rugged good looks, even after a night with no sleep. His hair was rumpled and he needed a shave, but it was his eyes she saw. They were filled with pain. *This isn't good*, said a voice somewhere in the back of her mind. *He should be laughing and telling me not to listen to absurd gossip.*

He reached out toward her but she shrank back.

"It's true, Julie. I do a lot of work for them."

"But not—" Her gaze darted around the cabin. "But not now. You're not working for them now, are you? Tell me you didn't come up here for them." She wondered if he could hear her heart breaking.

"I wish I could . . ." His voice trailed off. His hands clutched the wheel, knuckles white with tension. "They did ask me to come up here and check you out. I wanted to tell you, but—"

"But what?" She jumped to her feet. "But you were having too much fun stringing me along? Is that it?" Her voice was getting louder, but she didn't care. She was only vaguely aware that they were approaching the SunBird dock. "It's beginning to make sense now. You thought you'd have a little summer romance and, as an added bonus, find out where I'm vulnerable."

"No!" The single word shattered the predawn silence. "I came here to protect you. I was worried about what they would do, who they would send—"

"Oh no." She backed away. "The only thing you were worried about was losing your biggest customer."

"Julie, that's not true. Sweetheart, you've got to listen to me."

The houseboat bumped against the dock and she flung the gate open and jumped out, eager to be as far away from him as possible. "Don't you 'sweetheart' me." She stood on the dock, hands clenched at her sides. "I should have known better but I so wanted to believe in you." She turned away, then stopped. "I loved you, Quentin." She scarcely recognized her own voice. It had turned cold, emotionless. "I loved you more than you can possibly know, but now I want you off my property, and don't come back."

She ran across the grass and up the steps as if pursued. She had to get as far away from him as possible. She quietly let herself into the house, taking care not to wake Mike and Sharon and the kids. She'd left them a note last night and it still lay on the table. She crumpled it up and tossed it away, stumbling upstairs with a soft moan of pain. Leaving a pile of clothes on the bathroom floor, she stepped into the shower and let the water beat down, washing away the tears that streamed down her cheeks.

She crawled into bed and set the clock, surprised to see that it was only five-thirty. Her whole world had turned around in the space of half an hour, and she didn't think she could bear another minute.

The tantalizing aroma of coffee greeted her when she awoke two hours later. She swung her legs over the side of the bed, surprised that she'd been able to sleep at all.

Suddenly the memory of Quentin's treachery came flooding back and she doubled over, clutching at her stomach. She staggered into the bathroom and stared at herself in the mirror. Her eyes were dull and red-rimmed, mute reminders of her shattered dreams.

Get over it, kiddo, she told herself, and held a cold cloth to her eyes. *You've got a business to run and you can't afford to wallow in self-pity.* She brushed her hair until it shone, grateful for the natural curl that had never grown out.

Sharon greeted her in the kitchen. "I see you and Quentin managed to get the houseboat back." She passed Julie a cup of coffee. "I hope you don't mind, but the kids would like to head farther south and do some camping. We brought our gear, and they're dying to try it out."

Julie forced a bright smile. "That sounds like fun. Of course I don't mind." She desperately wanted to look out the front window but was afraid. "Can I give you a hand with anything?"

"Thanks, but no. We're ready to shove off." She looked up as Mike came in the back door. "I know it's your busy season, so we'll say good-bye now."

"Good-bye, Squirt."

Julie winced at the use of her nickname. The memories were too fresh. "Good-bye, Mike. See you soon, okay?"

"You bet. Hey, I couldn't find Callahan earlier, so I figured he's still asleep after your late night. Would you tell him for me not to wait so long next time?"

Julie swallowed. "Will do." She followed them out the door.

Jeremy and Nicole gave her quick hugs, then jumped in the backseat, eager to get under way. Mike tapped the horn twice and then they were gone.

Julie watched them disappear around the corner, her hand still raised in a wave. She stood there for several moments, listening to the leaves rustling in the morning breeze. If she didn't look, then it might have been a bad dream. But she knew better, and she also knew that the sooner she faced up to it, the sooner she could get on with the rest of her life.

With a pounding heart, she walked to the corner of the building and looked around the side. The spot where Quentin had parked his Mercedes was empty. *I will get through this*, she told herself, then headed for the dock, preparing herself for what she would say to Carl.

"Morning, Julie." Carl's expression was blank as he greeted her from the roof of *Osprey*. "Thanks for bringing her back. I'm draining the hot tub now, and Jenna says it won't take long to clean, since it was only out for a day. She'll be ready to rent again in a couple of hours." He slid down the ladder and stood on the back deck. "Quentin left me a note and the keys to *Chickadee*." He pulled them from his pocket. "He told me yesterday that he might be leaving soon, but I didn't realize it would be this quickly." He shrugged. "Now that we're back to full strength we don't really need him, but I enjoyed having him around." He held out the keys.

Julie stared at him mutely. He lifted up her hand and placed the keys in her palm, curling her fingers around them. "He's a good man, Julie," he said softly, patting her hand before going back to work.

Julie walked up the dock in a daze. Quentin had planned to leave early, and she'd known nothing about it! She hadn't thought it possible, but suddenly she felt worse. She paused at the foot of the stairs and took a deep breath. Time to face Maggie. She steeled herself for the encounter.

Her mouth fell open as she came through the door. Her friend was on the telephone as usual, but that was the only familiar thing about her today. Maggie's hair was a rich auburn shade, curling softly around a skillfully made-up face. She looked up and blushed as Julie stared at her.

"Yes, sir. We've just had a last-minute cancellation." Julie circled the desk, observing the changes in her friend. "Yes, your credit card number will hold the boat until four o'clock this afternoon." She turned to her computer and started entering the details of the rental. Her fingernails, although shorter than normal, were still painted a bright red, and Julie smiled. Some things never change.

"You look fabulous, Maggie. If I'd known how beautiful you'd be, I'd have dragged you down to that hair salon years ago." She looked at her friend with a critical eye. "That hair color is perfect. All right, what's the scoop?"

Maggie took off the headset and ran her fingers self-consciously through her hair. "It's time I started to look my age. Going out with Ivan made me see that." She grinned. "You could say we're an item."

Julie laughed and the tension drained from her body. "That's wonderful, Mags. I'm happy for you, I really am. Where was I all this time?"

"Sorry, Jules, but you were tied up with Mister Quentin Sexy Callahan." Her face grew serious. "And then with all that stuff about his father, and your family arriving, there just wasn't a good time to tell you." Her voice softened. "You'll like him, Julie. He's a logger, and he has his own truck. Like I said, his name is Ivan, and if you have a caricature of a logger in your mind, then that's him."

"You mean big and hunky and handsome? If you like him, he must be something special."

"Yeah." Maggie sighed. "He likes classical music, and I daresay he reads even more than I do." She turned suddenly. "I was hoping you and Quentin could come out to dinner with us while Nick is at camp. You know, a night out for the big kids."

Julie blinked back tears at the mention of Quentin's name.

"Julie, what is it?" Maggie looked from her friend to the dock, then back again. "Come to think of it, his car wasn't in the parking lot when I got here this morning." She rose and walked to the side window, waiting for her friend to speak. When Julie remained silent, she continued. "He's gone, isn't he?"

Julie nodded, then grabbed a tissue and dabbed at her eyes. "You were right all along. He works for Delahunt." She went to stand beside her friend. "He admitted that they sent him here."

"Oh, Julie, no. I wish I could think of something wise to say right now."

"Me too, but at least you didn't say 'I told you so.'" A tear slid down the side of her face, but she ignored it. She stared out the window at the dock, wishing Quentin would reappear, that he would tell her it had all been a terrible mistake. "I loved him, Maggie. I loved him so much."

Maggie slipped an arm around her shoulders. "I know you did, Julie. I only wish I could take away some of your pain."

Julie sniffled. "He even told Carl he was planning to leave, but did he tell me? Oh, no." She slipped out of Maggie's embrace. "You know, I think I'd like to be alone for a while. Maybe I'll just go and wander in the park or something."

"We only have one arrival today, so why not?" Maggie gave her friend a searching look. "Are you going to be all right?"

"Oh, yes," Julie replied. "I'll get over it. I'm just glad Nicky isn't here."

Maggie waited until she heard Julie go down the outside stairs, then watched her get into her car. "It's a good thing Quentin Callahan isn't here right now," she murmured to herself. "Or I'd give him a piece of my mind."

* * *

Julie drove around for a while, searching for somewhere she could be alone. Crowds of tourists thronged the beaches, and the downtown area hummed with shoppers. "That's it," she murmured, pulling into a shady spot by the park. The baseball diamond and the adjacent bleachers were deserted and, scarcely conscious of getting out of her car, she found herself sitting in the lowest row of the bleachers, elbows propped on the bench behind. The poplars behind the bleachers whispered among themselves as she tried to make sense of what had happened.

Chapter Thirteen

How had she allowed herself to fall so completely under Quentin's spell? Her eyes ran the bases as she recalled how their relationship had changed from one of friendship to one of love . . . at least on her part.

She hated to admit it, but she had only herself to blame. Sure, she'd warned him about not needing his help, about being independent. But when it came right down to it, she'd talked the talk but she hadn't walked the walk. He'd been very clever, making himself indispensable around the dock, slowly insinuating himself into her life and her heart. And Nick! She shut her eyes, visualizing Nick's return from camp. He'd hand her something he made in crafts, then run down to the dock, looking for his idol, full of stories. How could she tell him that Quentin had left, just like his father?

She gazed into the distance, her thoughts swirling. What exactly had Quentin ferreted out that would give Delahunt leverage in their attempts to buy her company? She couldn't think of a single thing. He had scarcely asked her about Apex Houseboats, even when she brought them up.

Of course he wouldn't, she told herself angrily. He already knew all about them. It was her operation he was interested in. Okay, so he'd worked with Carl and had observed the operation from that aspect, but that was all. She gnawed at her lower lip, trying to put together the pieces of the puzzle. Why hadn't he made more of an effort to come into the office, or to ask her about financial details? He hadn't done any of the things she'd expect if he were looking for flaws in her operation. No wonder she had been unwilling to confront him when Maggie reported his suspected connection with Delahunt.

She pressed her fingertips against her temples. She could rationalize his behavior, but the facts remained. He worked for Delahunt and had come at their request. And now he was gone, and he'd taken her heart with him.

Quentin pulled into a truck stop in Hope. He hadn't eaten since breakfast yesterday. He wasn't hungry, though he knew that he should eat. In the men's room he splashed water on his face and stared into the mirror. Bleary eyes looked back, and he rubbed his fingers on stubbled cheeks. Shaving could wait until he got home.

He slid into a booth and clasped a mug of coffee with both hands. How could he have made such a mess of things? He shook his head. He really didn't know.

The look on Julie's face had haunted him during the long drive. His experience in corporate boardrooms and in deciphering complex company structures didn't help one bit when it came to dealing with one beautiful—and independent—woman. He had known from the beginning that it was a mistake not to tell her about his duplicitous mission. He looked down at the ham and eggs the waitress placed before him. He didn't remember ordering them. He tried to eat, but the food stuck in his throat, and he pushed the plate away.

Why hadn't he been honest with Julie? The answer was simple—he had fallen for her the moment he'd seen her that first day. Or had he always loved her, somewhere in the back of his mind? Maybe that was why no other woman had measured up in all these years.

He took a drink of coffee and couldn't help but smile, recalling the fierce look in her eyes when she'd explained her need for independence. And so he'd taken the easy way out, not wanting to shatter their fragile relationship. Stupidity! That's what it was. Sheer stupidity on his part not to trust that she would understand why he had come.

He stood up abruptly and called for his check. He'd made a mess of things with Julie, but he would not be deterred from his original mission—to protect her. And if she could find a way to forgive him, he'd continue to do just that—for the rest of his life.

"Come on, Jules. You can't mope around here forever." As usual, Maggie didn't mince words. "It's just for a casual meal. I've met Bryan, and he's really nice."

Maggie could be a real nag sometimes. It was a good thing they were friends. "All right, all right. I'll come with you, but it's not a date with Bryan, okay? I'm simply joining my friend and her boyfriend."

"Atta girl. Wear that spaghetti strap number and those dynamite high-heeled sandals."

"And what kind of message would that send?" Julie rolled her eyes.

"If you've got it . . ."

"Yeah, yeah. But it just so happens I'm not in the mood to flaunt it."

"I know, kiddo." Maggie gave her an encouraging smile. "But I'm glad you're coming, and besides, it's high time you met Ivan."

The popular waterside restaurant was crowded when Julie arrived. She couldn't spot Maggie, but one of her friends was serving and motioned to the patio. "If you're looking for Maggie, she's out there with a couple of gorgeous hunks." She took in Julie's dress and high heels. "Although I don't think there'll be any leftovers. Too bad for me." She winked at Julie and turned to the table she was serving.

"Julie Chapman, I'd like you to meet Ivan Jensen. And this is Bryan Adams." Maggie beamed.

"Love your music," murmured Julie, sitting down next to the ruggedly handsome stranger. "Sorry, I guess that wasn't very original."

Dark green eyes smiled at her. "I've heard it before, but never from someone so beautiful."

Julie felt herself flush. She shouldn't have come, but she was determined to stick it out for Maggie's sake. She extended a hand to Ivan. "I'm delighted to meet you, Ivan. Anyone who can tame this woman has my admiration." Her small hand disappeared in his grasp.

"I didn't ask her to change a thing," he said, surprising her with the timbre of his voice. He sounded like a cross between Sean Connery and James Earl Jones. He took Maggie's hand. "I like her just the way she is."

A stab of jealousy caught her unaware, and she nodded her agreement. She was glad for Maggie, she really was, but her friend's happiness was such a contrast with her own dark thoughts.

"Would you like something to drink?" She was grateful when Bryan interrupted her musings.

"A Perrier would be nice, if it isn't too much trouble."

"Angie is swamped tonight. I'll go to the bar and get it." He stood up and she immediately noticed that he was the same height as Quentin. *Stop that*, she told herself. *You've only just arrived and you're already comparing them.* Bryan's slacks were crisply creased, and his shirt appeared new. He laughed as the bartender handed him the drink, and a row of even teeth flashed in his tanned face. Julie could hardly wait to get away.

"You were a barrel of laughs last night." Maggie greeted her the next morning with a worried expression.

"Was I really awful?" Julie wouldn't have embarrassed her friend for the world.

"Not really. Bryan kept asking questions about you after you left, so I think I was the only one who noticed that you weren't interested." She doodled on the scratch pad she kept on her desk. "He wants to call you, I think."

"Oh, Maggie." Julie rolled her head from side to side, trying to ease the tension in her neck. "I don't think it's a good idea to get involved with anybody right now. Even someone as perfect as Ivan's friend." She got up from her desk and walked to the picture window, arms crossed resolutely. "I keep thinking he's going to come back, Mags. I keep waiting for him to appear out of nowhere and tell me it was all a misunderstanding." She brushed away a tear.

"It's going to take a while to forget him, that's all. I hate to admit it, but I'm still in love with him."

She'd come home last night, crawled into bed, and let the tears flow. She'd been crying far too much since Quentin left, but she knew that eventually the pain would lessen. This morning when she awoke she was drained of energy, but she forced herself to get up. She had to get through this and be strong for Nick when he got home. She looked forward to the day when Quentin Callahan and Delahunt were nothing more than a distant memory.

Quentin sat nonchalantly in the chair facing Parker Henderson's desk while his biggest customer scanned the flimsy report.

"Are you serious, Callahan? With all your expertise, you couldn't find some chink in their armor?"

Quentin shook his head, his expression giving nothing away. Henderson had the eyes of a weasel, and he was relieved that he would not have to do business with him again. Beyond this present negotiation, that is.

"They simply don't want to sell. And from what I was able to ascertain, even if you did start a price war, they could probably outlast you. Their customer base is extremely loyal." Quentin was enjoying himself. He hadn't realized until this moment how much he disliked this company, but he had to keep his cool.

He waited for several beats. "I may have found an alternate solution for you, however."

"And what is that?" The CEO looked up. "I didn't see anything mentioned in your report." He flicked his fingers at the folder on the desk. "If you could call that a report."

"I think you should buy that piece of property about half

a mile down the Narrows. You could relocate your present structures, or build new ones, for that matter. As you so astutely pointed out, it's the land that's valuable."

"But—" The look on the CEO's face almost made up for Quentin's personal turmoil. "I told you we couldn't get a line on who owns it." He leaned across the desk. "We'd buy it in a New York minute if we had the chance."

"Well, the clock is running and the terms are reasonable."

Henderson's eyes narrowed and he glared across the expanse of desk. "Out with it, Callahan. What's the deal?"

"Three hundred feet of waterfront on Sicamous Narrows, right on 'Houseboat Row.'"

"How much?" It came out as a growl.

"It's a good deal, actually. A straight across the board swap. Your current location for the new one. Docks to stay in place, buildings negotiable, and you get your increased water frontage." Quentin sat back.

The CEO now resembled a fish. His mouth opened and closed as he tried to think and speak at the same time. "How did you find out who owns the property?"

Quentin reached down, picked up his briefcase, and extracted a file. He placed it on the edge of the massive desk. "Here, see for yourself."

Henderson reached for the file and scanned the documents. "Who is QC Holdings and why couldn't we find them?"

Quentin spread his hands. "It's me. And you couldn't find 'them' because I learned from the best." He grinned at the man across the desk. "Offshore companies aren't exactly a secret, you know."

The CEO sputtered. "You? You own that property?" He looked back at the file, his expression changing from anger to incredulity. "You've got it all figured out, haven't you?"

Quentin nodded. "Yes, I own the property and yes, I have it all figured out. I wouldn't bring you a proposal like this unless I had worked out the details. Oh, by the way, you get the report on SunBird for free. Let's just call it a bonus."

The CEO sat back in his chair, a faint smile on his face. "I've got to hand it to you, Callahan. Not very many people surprise me."

"I'll take that as a compliment."

Henderson didn't reply. He tapped the papers on his desk with a manicured fingernail. "Why are you doing this? You have a great business going. What could you possibly want with that Apex property?"

Quentin smiled. "It's a wedding gift for my wife."

Julie looked out the kitchen window just as Bruce pulled up with three tired campers. Looking slightly sunburned, Nick jumped down from the backseat and traipsed around to the trunk, where he pointed out his knapsack to Tommy's dad.

"Thanks, Mr. Shawcroft." He looked at Julie, and she had to steel herself not to run and throw her arms around him.

"Thank you, Bruce." She waved from the doorway and stepped aside as Nick came in. Going down on her knees, she gave him a quick hug, brushing his hair back from his eyes. "Did you have fun?" His arms were studded with mosquito bites, but otherwise he appeared intact.

"Yeah, it was excellent. They have two new canoes this year, and we got to spend lots of time in them." He rummaged around in his knapsack. "I made you something," he said, frowning as he felt around in the bottom of the bag.

"Here they are." With a flourish, he presented her with two leather coasters. "I made them myself." He pointed to the designs, which Julie assumed were fish. "That's called tooling," he said proudly. "I made one for you and one for Maggie."

Julie fought back tears. "They're perfect, Nick. I think Maggie is still in the office. Shall we go down and surprise her?"

"Okay." Nick ran ahead down the stairs and by the time Julie caught up, Maggie was admiring the gift.

"Guess what, Mom?" Nick ran to the window and looked toward the dock. "I passed my senior swimmers test." He turned to Julie, a puzzled expression on his face. "Where is Quentin? I want to show him my badge." He headed for the door.

Julie shot a pained look at Maggie. "He isn't there, Nicky. He's gone back to Vancouver."

The youngster paused, absorbing the information. "That's okay," he said, looking up at her with a confident smile. "He'll be back."

Maggie turned away, and Julie felt a lump form in her throat. How was she going to explain? She went over to the window and placed a hand on his shoulder. "I don't think so, Nicky. He left a few days ago."

The brown eyes looked up at her. "But he'll be back, Mom. I asked him if he had to leave and he told me yes, but that he would be back." His gaze darted toward Maggie, then came back to rest on Julie. "He promised."

Julie's heart broke as her son left the office and ran back upstairs. "How am I going to handle this?" she asked. "He's convinced that Quentin is coming back." She wanted to believe right along with Nick, but was afraid to climb onto that rollercoaster again.

Maggie seemed to read her thoughts. "Now don't go getting yourself all worked up, Jules. You know how kids are. Maybe he heard what he wanted to hear."

Julie set the coaster down on her desk, running her fingers over the incised design. Maggie was right, but a tiny spark of hope still glimmered in a corner of her heart, waiting to be fanned into flames.

"You're right, Maggie, but I've got to hope." She followed Nick upstairs. "I'll see you tomorrow."

The following day was hectic but Julie thrived on busy days like this. Her staff worked smoothly together, cleaning and servicing the boats, and assisting the new arrivals. At five-thirty, she slumped into the seat of an ATV, her back sore from prepping boats. "Well, we managed to get them all off," she said with a satisfied smile. "This is the first time in ages that I can remember every boat being rented out at the same time."

Carl removed his tool belt. "And only two coming back tomorrow. I like that." His gaze wandered to *Chickadee*. "We could have used Quentin today. He fit in so smoothly around here, I hadn't realized how much he accomplished in a day."

"He accomplished a lot, all right. He made Nick believe that he's coming back." Her brow creased with worry. "How am I going to tell him it isn't true?"

"Julie." Carl took a step toward her. "Quentin *is* coming back. He told me as well, the same day you two went to pick up *Osprey*."

Julie stared at him, processing this new information. "Well, he seems to have told everybody but me." She gave a weak, self-conscious laugh. "Although I know it's not about me. He obviously meant that he'd be coming back to see his father."

Carl gave her an odd look, then changed the subject. "I thought I'd do an overhaul on *Chickadee* tonight. She's a good boat, and since we're so busy I thought Maggie could put her into the database and we could rent her out. What do you think?"

Julie looked at the little houseboat. "Why not?" *Chickadee* was a constant reminder of Quentin and it would be a relief to have it out of sight. She glanced at her watch. "My goodness, Nick has a ball game tonight, and I'm supposed to drive him." She walked off, murmuring to herself. "I wonder what Nick will think if I wander off and listen to music while his game's on. I think he'll forgive me for one night."

Quentin chafed at the traffic as he drove through the Okanagan Valley en route to Sicamous. He scarcely noticed the dry, sage-covered hills give way to lush green growth as he drew nearer to Sicamous. His mind was on Julie, and he was surprised to realize that he was nervous.

He glanced at the briefcase in the passenger seat and smiled. His gift for organization had served him well when it came time to expedite the property swap, and the title to Apex's present location was tucked into an envelope inside the briefcase. The negotiations had been straightforward: they would pay rent for the use of the property for the balance of the season while they began construction on their new site. That part had been accomplished fairly easily. Now all he had to do was convince Julie.

The parking lot was almost full. License plates from as far away as Tennessee attested to the popularity of the region. Every slip on the dock was vacant. Every one except *Chickadee*, that is. He wandered onto the grass and noticed a slight tilt as someone moved around inside the houseboat. He stepped onto the dock.

"Hello, Carl."

The maintenance chief looked up in surprise. "Hello, yourself." He glanced up toward the house, then his gaze came back to rest on Quentin. "Good to see you. How was the trip?"

"I managed to accomplish everything I wanted." It was Quentin's turn to look toward the house. "Is Julie around?"

"No. She took Nick to a baseball game." Carl eyed him curiously.

"Well, if you don't mind, I'll go and find her." He grinned. "I have some explaining to do."

"You might check the bandstand area," Carl called to Quentin's retreating back. "She said something about going over there while the game was on."

Quentin waved in acknowledgment and kept walking.

Julie positioned herself on the knoll overlooking the bandstand. Faint shouts from the direction of the baseball diamond mingled with the discordant sounds of the musicians tuning up. Exhausted by the tug-of-war going on inside her head, she scarcely heard the announcement as the spokesman lifted the microphone.

"Good evening, ladies and gentlemen, and welcome to our Concert in the Park series. Tonight is for all you lovers out there." Julie groaned. "We're going to play some oldies, and we'd like to start our program with one of the most beautiful love songs ever written. Ladies and gentlemen, 'When I Fall in Love.' "

The familiar notes drifted through the air, weaving their magic spell. Julie closed her eyes, wondering if it were possible for her heart to shatter into even smaller pieces. Heedless of anyone around her, she closed her eyes and lost herself in the music, tears rolling down her face.

"Don't cry, sweetheart." Memories of Quentin were so distinct she could almost hear his voice. "They're playing our song."

Slowly, as though coming out of a dream, she opened her eyes. He was at her side, blurred and out of focus. "Quentin?" she whispered. "Is that you?"

He removed a handkerchief from his pocket and dabbed at her tears. The love shining from his eyes was unmistakable, and she sat very still as he brushed his lips against hers. "It's me," he said, touching her cheek with his fingertips. "I love you, Julie, and I'll never forgive myself for causing you pain." He stood up and offered her his hand. "Will you let me explain?"

She put her hand in his, her heart beating so wildly that she was sure he could hear it.

"Before we go, there's something I have to do." He looked at her intently.

"What's that?"

"This." He slipped his hands into her hair, gazing into her eyes with infinite tenderness. He lowered his lips to hers, kissing her with a sweetness and longing that left her breathless. Her arms went around his neck, and his mouth caressed hers, reconfirming what she already knew. He had come home to stay.

She pulled back. "They say this song is for lovers." Her eyes searched his face. "Is that us?"

He pulled her head to his chest, and she heard his heart hammering. "Forever," he murmured. "That's how long I'll love you, Julie."

Julie looked up in surprise as the server came to offer refills. Where had the time gone? Quentin's story had spilled out over coffee, and she'd listened in amazement.

"So, you found them another piece of property, and they're going to start building right away?"

"That's what they say. It seemed the best way to get them off your back. They'll be gone by next spring." He reached across the table and took her hand. "I was only trying to protect you, Julie. But instead, I hurt you, and I'm genuinely sorry for that. If I could do it all over again, I'd lay my cards on the table right away." He gave her a rueful grin. "You were so darned independent."

"I was, wasn't I?" She looked at her watch. "Oh, my goodness. The ball game will be over. We'd better run."

The teams were still on the field when they pulled up at the baseball diamond. Tommy's dad was standing beside the bleachers, and they joined him.

"What inning is it?" Julie asked.

"Bottom of the tenth. Score is tied, two down, two on base, and Nick's at bat."

"Oh, my gosh." Julie's hand flew to her mouth.

The pitcher wound up and lobbed one at Nick. To Julie's eyes, his swing seemed to happen in slow motion. The sweet sound of the ball connecting with a wooden bat rang out as Nick hit a long fly ball into right field. He flew around the bases and came around home plate standing up, to the cheers of his teammates.

Julie and Quentin cheered louder than anyone else, and Nick's eyes lit up as he spotted them. He ran up to Quentin, and they exchanged high fives.

"Did you see me, Quentin? Did you see?" Nick vibrated with excitement.

"I sure did, and you were great." Quentin looked down at the youngster with obvious affection.

"See, I told you, Mom." He stood close to Quentin, a proprietary smile on his face. "I told you he'd come back."

They agreed to meet back at SunBird, and Julie regretfully parted from Quentin.

Nick glanced at her from time to time as they drove home. "I guess you're happy, huh, Mom? I mean about Quentin coming back?"

Julie didn't try to hide her smile. "Yes, Nicky. I'm very happy."

"I wonder what Quentin wants? He told us to meet him down at the dock."

They pulled into the parking lot and she turned to her son. "Let's go and see."

Chapter Fourteen

Quentin was already on the dock when they arrived, studying the shoreline and the adjacent docks. Most of Apex's houseboats were out this evening. He turned as they walked toward him.

"What's up?" Julie looked at him curiously. "Why did you want to meet here?"

"I brought you a gift." He handed her the envelope.

"What is it?" She scanned the document and frowned, then read it a second time. Her eyes widened. "Is this what I think it is?"

Quentin nodded.

"It's clear title to their property, and it's in my name." She looked at him, dumbfounded. "I don't understand. How did you get them to agree to this?"

He raised his eyebrows. "I traded them. My property, farther down the Narrows, in exchange for theirs. It was a deal they couldn't refuse."

It took a moment for his words to sink in. "You owned that property?"

"Yup. I started paying for it nine years ago."

A slow smile crept over her face. "You're unbelievable, Quentin Callahan." She held out the papers. "But why this?"

"It's a wedding present." His eyes held hers.

"But—" She looked back down at the document in her trembling hands. "I'm not getting married."

He stepped forward and tilted up her chin. "I was hoping to change that. I love you, Julie. I've loved you from the moment I saw you on your hands and knees, a paintbrush in your hand." He pulled Nick to his side. "Will you marry me, Jules? That is, if Nick approves."

Nick looked at his mother, who had a goofy smile on her face. "Do you love him, Mom?"

"I think I've always loved him, Nicky."

"And how about you, Quentin? Are you going to stick around?"

Quentin smiled at the youngster's negotiating skills. "I'm back to stay this time, Nick. And I love you both."

Nick grinned and looked from his mom to the man he admired. "That sounds pretty good to me." He started to walk back to the house and then ran back to where the two adults stood, their hands linked. "I got my swimming badge, Quentin. Thanks for the help."

"I never doubted it."

"Yeah. Well, I think I'll leave you guys to kiss and stuff like that." He ran across the lawn and up the stairs to the house.

"You heard him." Quentin reached for her. "We're supposed to kiss and stuff like that."

Julie went willingly into the circle of his arms. "Sounds good to me," she murmured, and lifted her lips to receive his kiss. They had both come home.